GRIFFIN'S
LEGACY

GRIFFIN'S LEGACY

by N.R. Rose

TATE PUBLISHING
AND ENTERPRISES, LLC

Griffin's Legacy
Copyright © 2013 by N.R. Rose. All rights reserved.

No part of this publication may be reproduced, stored in a retrieval system or transmitted in any way by any means, electronic, mechanical, photocopy, recording or otherwise without the prior permission of the author except as provided by USA copyright law.

This novel is a work of fiction. Names, descriptions, entities, and incidents included in the story are products of the author's imagination. Any resemblance to actual persons, events, and entities is entirely coincidental.

The opinions expressed by the author are not necessarily those of Tate Publishing, LLC.

Published by Tate Publishing & Enterprises, LLC
127 E. Trade Center Terrace | Mustang, Oklahoma 73064 USA
1.888.361.9473 | www.tatepublishing.com

Tate Publishing is committed to excellence in the publishing industry. The company reflects the philosophy established by the founders, based on Psalm 68:11,
"The Lord gave the word and great was the company of those who published it."

Book design copyright © 2013 by Tate Publishing, LLC. All rights reserved.
Cover design by Joana Quilantang
Interior design by Honeylette Pino
Illustrations by Kenny Abigae Badana

Published in the United States of America

ISBN: 978-1-62746-586-1
1. Fiction / Fantasy / Epic
2. Fiction / Action & Adventure
13.10.01

TABLE OF CONTENTS

A Note from the Author 7

Chapter 1:   The Dark Ones 13
Chapter 2:   Among Them 23
Chapter 3:   Breaking Daylight 35
Chapter 4:   The Single Egg 45
Chapter 5:   The Return 57
Chapter 6:   Awakening 63
Chapter 7:   Griffin's Bow 71
Chapter 8:   The Burns 79
Chapter 9:   The Celebration 91
Chapter 10: Molidon 105
Chapter 11: Help from the Human World . . . 115
Chapter 12: A Last Resort 123
Chapter 13: Captured by His Own Kind 137

Chapter 14: An Unexpected Encounter.... 145
Chapter 15: The Results 153
Chapter 16: Dragons........................ 163
Chapter 17: An Explanation.................175
Chapter 18: Dream Visions..................187
Chapter 19: Taking Action 203
Chapter 20: Scales...........................211
Chapter 21: Let There be Light............. 217
Chapter 22: A New Kind of Flight.......... 227
Chapter 23: Fight for Our Existence........ 233
Chapter 24: The Last Riddle 253
Chapter 25: Liberty in Aranwea............ 273

A NOTE FROM THE AUTHOR

Writing the *Griffin's Calling Trilogy* has been a rewarding journey for the past six years. It has been an incredible era of my life. Just as anything that is worthwhile, writing this novel has had its ups and downs that I wouldn't trade for anything. As I began hand writing the first novel, *Griffin's Calling,* late at night in my bedroom, I had not the slightest ounce of knowledge that it would turn into a trilogy. To me, in the beginning, writing this story was a way for me to escape. I have always admired the fantasy genre whether it was in books, movies, plays, or video games, but creating something such as this was an experience unlike any other. When I picked up that pencil to jot down the words of my first ever novel, I was immediately living and breathing in the world I was creating. I felt the joy and pain in each and every one of my characters. When they hurt, I felt this emotion. When they conquered their most profound challenge, I was there, celebrating with them. I know each person in my novels as if they were my closest friends. They will forever be a part of me.

I recently completed my four years in college at California State University, Fresno, and there my passion for athletics was pushed to its extreme limits. I was offered the amazing opportunity to play lacrosse at Fresno State, a Division 1 program. Along with my passion for writing, sports have been an even longer passion. Sports have been a part of me for my entire life. I never thought these two aspects of my life would collide in the way that they did. It turns out that if you are a college athlete receiving a scholarship, you are not allowed to do certain things. Well, one of those things just so happened to not mix so smoothly with being an author. When I first came in as a freshman at Fresno State, my first novel was just getting released. I showed my coach at the time, and the Fresno State Athletic Department, one of the first copies of *Griffin's Calling*. They all thought it was very exciting, but there was one problem. That problem was that I had my real name on the cover of the book, instead of a pen name. After the school had evaluated the situation, they told me that it was against the rules to have my real name on the novels until I was done being a student athlete. They also told me that I would not be able to play or practice with my team until I had a pen name. The worst part at the time was I was not allowed to even claim the novels as mine, even if I had a pen name, until I was done being a student athlete. I was devastated. I was shattered with not only the fact that I was banned from playing lacrosse for the time being, but also that I couldn't even promote my novels for four whole years. Even though this was going on, I knew I couldn't let it bring me down. My family and I came up with the pen name N. R. Rose. Tate Publishing was extremely accommodating to changing my name on my novels, and it wasn't but a few weeks later I could play again. Still upset with not being able to promote my novel, my parents helped me realize that I could use this time to solely focus on my schooling, and being the best athlete I could be. Now that these four years have finally come to an end, I am immensely saddened that I will no longer be playing lacrosse, but I am ready for the next chapter of my life. This next chapter is finally, at last, being able to promote myself as a young adult novelist.

I am blessed and thankful for the many people who have helped me along the way. I have had various friends and family members that have never stopped believing in my writing career and me. My teammates at Fresno State have given me endless support and reinforcement with my novels and always kept me in good spirits. And without the help and encouragement from my parents, Michelle and Mike Harrington, this trilogy would not have been conceivable. No matter what was going on in their lives, they were always there to offer a helping hand with my novels. Whether it was bouncing ideas off of each other, or gaining different opinions and scenarios to come up with, they always made time for Griffin and me. Mike and Michelle Harrington know this trilogy inside and out better than anyone else (besides me, of course). They have been here since that sixteen-year-old girl presented them with a notebook full of ideas. And now, six years later, they are still here. Only that girl is now twenty-two and has a four-year degree in Communications, four years completed in college athletics, and three published novels. I want to thank them for all of these things I have accomplished, for without them, it would not have been possible. Thank you, Mom and Dad.

THE DARK ONES

What can bring someone or something so much darkness? What is it that drives a being to contain nothing but merciless hatred? Hatred, combined with the intent of no mercy, is one combination for destruction. These characteristics are found in nothing other than the Shriekian. These creatures live with one intention in mind and one intention only—the will to dominate and multiply. They linger in the murky depths of the Shriekian domain in the land of Aranwea.

However, the Shriekian did not use to be such vile animals, and at one time they use to live in harmony with the other beings that existed in Aranwea.

The rising of their leader, Cyrus, began the alteration of this kind. Cyrus believed in total power. He had great leadership qualities and charismatic values that could convince fire and water into being allies. Had he used his power for good, he would have done wonderful things for the land of Aranwea. Had he used his abilities to create a harmonizing atmosphere, the land in which they lived would not be in complete, utter war. This single leader was able to convince his kind, the Shriekian, to believe that they were the superior race, and that all others who opposed them, or were not like them, were nothing more than vermin. This had been their intent for many decades now, and even though Cyrus was no longer in power, his legacy still lived within them.

A new leader of the Shriekian had been born. He was a leader like none of them had ever thought would exist in their community. It was a leader that was not of their kind. They had raised this being since he was young. He grew up with the Shriekian, learning their ways and what his role would be living with them. And in doing so, his mind-set was not only changed into the ways of the Shriekian, but they made him master of their kind, the commander of their army. Ever since this creature had come to power, they had rapidly grown stronger. This being went by the name of Gotham and was not born from the Shriekian family, but from the family of the lost dragons. Gotham was one of the two dragons that had been seen in Aranwea in the past five decades. The rest of the dragons had suddenly gone missing, never to be seen since.

The Shriekian treated Gotham as if he were their god. He had the same charismatic values that Cyrus once had. This was no surprise because Cyrus had raised Gotham as his own when Cyrus found him at a very young age. Gotham had wandered near the lake where the castle of the Shriekian domain rested. The black walls of the castle rose above the surface of the lake as the terrified young dragon witnessed such a scene. The drawbridge collapsed in the water, causing a wave to crash on shore. Out of the castle doors emerged a decrepit eel-like being. It had round black eyes the shape of large eggs and a thin slippery body. It jumped in the water, swimming smoothly up to the young dragon called Gotham. It sneered, "You can come with me, or you can die like the rest of your kind. Now, young dragon, what say you?"

From then on, the dragon learned to live with the Shriekian. Although the dragon could not breathe underwater like the rest of them could, the Shriekian found a way around this. They invented a way to seal off specific rooms in the castle when their domain was submerged. This way Gotham could live among them. Cyrus instilled in Gotham's mind that he would be a great leader someday. He told him that if he believed in his will, he would deem him leader of all Shriekian and that one day all would bow down to him. The idea of power attracted this dragon. What Gotham did not realize was that when he agreed to live as a Shriekian, there would be no turning back.

You see, the Shriekian have a nearly undeniable power about them. They can insert appealing thoughts and ideas into the minds of others who are not of their kind. They had been born with a gift, or more of a curse. And that curse was the ability to tantalize others who were not like them. They instilled evil into others' minds without the victim being aware of it. That is why Gotham was one of them now—and forever shall be. To show their honor toward Gotham, the Shriekian created an emblem to wear around their neck. It was a metal piece made into a necklace with the symbol of a dragon on it. This signified their worthiness to their leader, Gotham. Down in the shadowy lake of the Shriekian domain, these creatures dwelled. The enemy had been growing stronger and multiplying with every day that passed, making their army more than just a force to reckon with but a nearly unstoppable force.

Even though these dreadful beings dwelled in their waters, they could survive on land as well. This gave them an unparalleled advantage. Many hundreds of years ago, the clan of the Shriekian used to only be able to exist in water for if they didn't, they would decease. It had the same effect as a fish flopping desperately on land. This was a limitation for these creatures because the other beings that lived in Aranwea did not live underwater. They were land animals. If the Shriekian wanted to rule the whole existence of Aranwea, they had to figure out a way to live, breath, and *walk* out of the water. With nothing but a tailfin, this would not be possible.

So the transformation began. Every time a new set of Shriekian eggs had been laid, the leaders of their kind would insert a poisonous substance into them. Many eggs were lost in this process. But these immoral creatures did not care, and only had one thing in mind— supremacy. It took many months for them to find the exact element that would allow them to grow two slimy legs once leaving water. And even though the Shriekian leaders who preformed this act knew that they would never see a pair of legs of their own, they did this for the generations to come. They did this so they could rule both land and water, and in doing so, they could kill off all others who inhabited this land.

The other animals that lived in this peaceful land were delighted once they found out that the Shriekian could now walk on land. They had no quarrels with the idea of now sharing the land with another species. This worked to the Shriekians' advantage for they were seen as trustworthy. They seemed as though they could live in harmony, but this was a horrid misconception for these loathsome beings had much different things in mind. And when the other creatures of Aranwea least expected it, when the Shriekian had them right where they wanted them, they attacked, showing no remorse or mercy. They slaughtered all that stood before them as long as they did not have Shriekian blood coursing through their veins. They were able to kill off nearly every other race that lingered in Aranwea, every other race—except for one.

This exceptional species was the Critins. And even though much of the Critins had been lost to the Shriekian, there was still an assembly of them who knew better than to ever trust the Shriekian. And ever since then, the family of the Critins had been desperately trying to hang on to their continuation. They had been able to prosper due to an exceptional person. This being was not like the Critins either. He was a human boy and went by the name of Griffin, Griffin Dominic. After being taken away from the human world into the land of Aranwea by Sable (the diamond bearer of the Critins) and Mogol (the dust keeper), the boy had found out he was of much greater importance than he expected. He was the answer to this race's prayers and the only one who could accomplish the prophecy and finally determine the Shriekians' weakness.

Griffin had sacrificed himself by leaving with the Shriekian many months ago. He did this during an attack on the Critin village in hopes they would depart. And they did. Even though the boy had overcome their last temptation against them, he pretended as though he was willing to go with them, and in doing so, he had bought the Critins a little more time to grow stronger. The Shriekian had not the slightest idea that Griffin was strong enough to overcome them. They thought that they had Griffin under *their* control, their management, but the Shriekian were vastly mistaken.

AMONG THEM

There he lay in a small confined room with white walls surrounding him like an enclosed insane asylum. Griffin Dominic dwelled in the Shriekian domain, many feet beneath the water's surface. The room was sealed from all water as the whole castle sat submerged. Hoping, enduring, and suffering, the boy rested on the cool cement flooring. He had lost count of the days spent with the Shriekian and had recently began to lose touch with reality. For a split moment, he would see her—Adria, that is. He would imagine Adria sitting under the trees with him, at the training ground, her smooth brown hair glistening in the sunlight and her eyes like infinite pools of fresh springwater. She would be there for a moment but then would be gone, and the disoriented boy would be alone once again, waiting for help to come—or waiting for the end to come. *Why haven't they found me yet?* Griffin would ask himself.

The Shriekian would visit the boy daily. They presented him with a foggy bowl of water and nearly raw fish that would cause him to be ill after almost every meal. And still Griffin hung on. He clung onto every bit of hope he could conjure—his Critin family—John, Snolan, Adria. This is what helped him hang on, but with the state he was in, Griffin knew very well that his body was not going to allow him to hang on much longer. His dark-brown hair was tattered and had grown well past his ears and down his neck. His once-vibrant blue eyes had grown shadowy and dull and had developed dark bags under them. Griffin's back contained imprinted scars where the Shriekian dug in their razor-like claws. If the boy desired to see the light of day again, he had to act without delay.

Griffin awoke in the morning with a large pounding in his head. It caused him to stand up abruptly, and when he opened his eyes, he saw nothing. He could only see pure and absolute blackness like a blind man.

"What's going on!" Griffin shouted, his words bouncing off the walls in the condensed room. Making a fist in either hand, he rubbed his eyes continuously for a few moments. Opening his blue eyes once more, he could still not see a thing. The boy could feel tears intensifying and anxiety pounding at his heart like a drummer in a rock-and-roll band. The boy fell to his knees and started to weep. "Get me out of here!" He began to thrash about the room slamming his fists against the wall. Suddenly a loud snap came from his left hand as he thrust it against the cement wall. "Owwwww!" the boy bellowed. As moments passed, his hand swelled greatly, inserting sharp pain throughout it. Griffin embraced his throbbing hand with the other one and sobbed in utter darkness.

As the boy rocked back and forth, caressing his injured hand, he began to see something.

It was nothing that was in front of the boy or in the room. Griffin was seeing visions. He had gained a gift by defying the Shriekians' last attempt to bring him to their side. He had overcome their last temptation many months ago, and by doing so, Griffin had been given the gift of foresight. Even though he had not had these revelations appear in his mind since he started the journey to the oldest griffin, he knew exactly what was occurring. "Please," Griffin whispered aloud, "help me get out of this place...help me find my way out."

In his mind, Griffin saw a hallway leading out of the room he was captured in. This hallway was not very long, and at the end of it was what looked to be a deep, large pool of water. His vision took him beneath this pool of water and revealed to him a tunnel, a large and lengthy waterway. Along the underpass were different turns presented; however, Griffin's vision kept him fixed on a specific path. It deviated left and right, taking different twists and turns. And then a light could be seen toward the surface. The surface was rapidly approaching until the water was broken free and the rich green forest could be seen from outside the lake. And as soon as the vision was brought on, it had disappeared, leaving Griffin able to see once again. "This is my way out." The boy stammered. He stood up hastily, " This is my way out!" Griffin's gift from defeating the Shriekians' last temptation had helped him once more. He now knew that there was hope, and there was in fact a way to escape the Shriekian domain.

Griffin replayed the vision over in his head time and time again. He recalled each and every turn the image had presented to him and ingrained it into his mind. This was not an impossible task for him to accomplish for he was quite familiar with memorizing the various paths in his backyard woods that he grew up in. The difficult part was not trying to remember the exact route that the vision took him on. This would be the easy part for him.

The task that would present itself as problematic would be getting out of this forsaken room in which he was being held hostage. The

Shriekian visited the boy once a day, bringing him undesirable food and musty water. There used to be two of these creatures arriving each day to tend to him, but more recently, they had let their guard down and only had one go to him. This would work in Griffin's favor. If he could bring down this lone Shriekian and close the room door behind him, he would be able to pursue the passageway, but he would need some kind of weapon. When Griffin had sacrificed himself to the Shriekian many months prior, he had left his shortbow and quiver of arrows behind for if he did not, the Shriekian would not believe that he had come to their side *willingly*. The only thing the stranded boy possessed was a whistle used to call on Snolan, a dragon and guardian of the Critin castle.

The next challenge Griffin would have to endure was being able to hold his breath underwater throughout the entire waterway and up to the surface of the lake. Also, with his now-throbbing hand, he would not be able to swim as efficiently as he normally would. Griffin practiced holding his breath for as long as he possibly could. Cheeks puffed to full length and face turning a dark purple, fifty seconds had passed, and he let out a large mouthful of air. Taking in great heaves of oxygen, he regained his composure. *Will this be long enough?* he eagerly pondered. Taking in many more breaths of air, Griffin tried once more. This time, he had gained fifteen more seconds. "This will have to do. I will not sit here and rot in this room. This is my only chance," he said aloud.

Back in the innermost part of the Shriekian domain, where the water also was sealed, two of the dreadful creatures were squabbling among one another. "I fed the little parasite last time! It's your turn, Clythe!"

The two angry Shriekian stared into each other's black eyes, their sharp teeth revealed, and slimy webbed claws clenched. The one called Clythe moved its rubbery body closer to the other Shriekian. "Oh yeah! Well who's going to make me?"

He shoved a small bowl of slop into the hands of Clythe. This dish was the intended meal for the boy. "You do it! It makes me nauseous to be around a human. It is *not* my job. Besides, the human is worthless. I do not know why I don't just do away with him right now!"

"*Enough!*" a deafening roar came from around the corner. Both Shriekian stopped their hostility and spun around abruptly. Turning the corner was a creature so large, so ominous, that even the Shriekian would shudder at such a sight. "What seems to be the problem here?" The being's voice was profound and demanding. It had beautiful black scales that consumed its entire body and two sharp horns jutting out from atop its head. The creature was about thirty feet in length, including its spiked tail, and stood decisively on all fours. Its bat-like wings were folded firmly by its side.

"G...G...Gotham...sir! We did not mean to cause a commotion!" the other Shriekian, named Wretch, stuttered.

The enormous dragon walked closer to the uneasy Shriekian. "I do not care *who* tends to the human. And if that dull mind of yours has so easily forgotten, we are keeping the boy alive because he is going to help us seize the diamond!" Gotham took in great volumes of air through his enlarged nostrils. "The Critins trust this boy. He is in our command now, and at the right moment, we will use this to our advantage. We need that red diamond!"

Both of the cowering Shriekian nodded their marine-like heads up and down in agreement.

"You are right, sir! I'll take care of it right away!" Wretch dashed off in the other direction of the castle with the bowl of mush sloshing in his hands.

The Shriekian castle was large and consumed a great amount of the lake. The walls of the domain had thick green sludge clinging about it, and it reeked of decaying oysters and fish. These parts of the castle were all linked together and sealed off from all water due to the issue that nether Griffin nor Gotham could survive in the underwater parts of the domain.

Wretch muttered to himself, "I always have to do the dirty work. I tell you what, it should be more than just Clythe and I tending to this nuisance!" The enraged being approached the door to Griffin's prison. He slammed his slippery hand onto the gray button that would slide the door upward and would allow him to enter the room.

Wretch found something he did not expect. He took one step into the room and saw Griffin lying on the floor facedown. The boy had one arm sprawled out to his side, and the other was tucked underneath his body. He was motionless and did not look as though a single breath was being taken into his body.

"Ha!" the creature chuckled. "Looks like I won't have to tend to this pest after all! The boy is deceased!" The Shriekian was now ranting and hopping up and down in enjoyment. He crept over to the immobile boy and poked him with his webbed toe. He stood over Griffin as green sludge dripped onto him and down the boy's back. Now curious, Wretch knelt down to the boy's side and started sniffing him. "I wonder how a human would taste...the last good meal I had was *all* those eggs at the Critin castle." These horrifying words had barely left the beast's mouth when Griffin sprang up and thrust the sharp whistle through the animal's alien-like eyeball.

"That's for the babies of Aranwea!" Griffin shouted, tears rising and anger setting in. Wretch roared in agony when Griffin pulled the whistle back out of its eye, and he crashed to the floor shrieking in pain. Griffin began to kick the vile thing in its stomach causing it to cough and convulse. Griffin stopped and stared at the suffering Shriekian, who was now oozing a black substance from his eye. The boy then turned to make his way out of the room.

"But it is impossible!" Wretch coughed. "You are under our control! *Our* temptation!"

Before shutting the door behind him, Griffin turned to face him one last time and spoke. "I was *never* under your temptation." Griffin then slammed his fist against the gray button, sealing the creature in the room and leaving it to suffer in solitude.

BREAKING DAYLIGHT

Griffin wiped the black sludge off his wooden whistle with his ratted green T-shirt. The Shriekian he had taken down by driving the whistle through its eye had left a mucky substance about it. Placing the whistle securely in his right front pocket, the boy walked down the hallway. Griffin gagged at the smell of the walls around him; he could barely make it through the corridor without vomiting for the odor was getting stronger as he pressed on. A few moments had passed, and the vision that Griffin saw had proved itself correct. He stopped at the ledge of a shadowy body of water.

"This is the waterway!" Griffin gasped. "This is my way out!" For a few seconds Griffin recalled the various twists and turns his vision had shown him. Although he did this, he did not waste time for he did not know how much longer he had before the Shriekian would catch wind that he had escaped. So without a moment's hesitation, he plunged into the ominous dark waters.

Griffin emerged quickly to the surface to gain one last breath. He coughed and choked as the green lake water slipped into his mouth like an uninviting leech. He profusely spit the water out and looked below him as he waded in the water. As his head was the only part of his body out of the dark water, he could see nothing beneath him.

In hope to gain some confidence in what he was about to do, Griffin thought back to his home—his home with the Critins. He remembered the sweet victory at the Shriekian domain nearly a year ago. He recalled the first night flight he had taken with his protector and beloved friend, Snolan. Before he sacrificed himself to the Shriekian many months prior, he evoked the memory of Sable stating that he thought of Griffin as a son. All these significant memories gave Griffin something. They gave this boy a gift that was far greater than any human, animal, or any being could derive. And this gift was the gift of hope.

With these thoughts racing through his head like flash photography, Griffin took in deep breaths. He calmed himself in doing so, and when he could contain no more air within himself, he drove his head underneath the cloudy water. He swam along the straight passageway. Plants that looked like seaweed passed him by as he kept along at a steady pace. Adrenaline shot through his veins, which helped ease the pain of his throbbing knuckle as he pulled through the water, and pushed his body forward. Once again, his foresight had proven correct, and he took a right turn through the murky water. Griffin kicked his legs and brought his arms through the water as efficiently as possible in hopes to not exhaust himself. He had never been a horrible swimmer, and growing up, the boy enjoyed taking trips to the local river with a couple of his only friends. However, Griffin's body was highly malnourished, and with every extension of his body through the water, he grew weary.

Griffin came to a division in the waterway. The vision had led him to take another right turn, but on the left, Griffin could make out something that sent a compulsion of vengeance through his core. Griffin did not go right; instead, he swam slightly down the left waterway and stopped. Floating before him sat a colony of what appeared to be frog eggs—Shriekian eggs. They were surrounded in a gooey matter that held them all together. In each green egg, there was a body of a small Shriekian. The creatures were rolled up in a ball with their eyes shut. Some had matured faster than the others and had sprouted small tail fins and webbed fingers. Others were still in their first stages of life and looked like nothing more than a large worm.

Harsh thoughts struck Griffin's mind as he moved his arms up and down through the water before the eggs. He remembered what these vile animals did to *their* Critin eggs. He remembered the memorial they had for the babies of Aranwea and the grave that rested in the Critin village for them. Griffin thought about thrashing his hands through the eggs' soft shells and causing whatever destruction he could to them. There was a flame of revenge that had been set to fire in his eyes and the boy swam up closer to the stagnant offspring. He gazed into the round thick substance that held them. Just before thrusting his fist through it, Griffin stopped himself.

He discontinued his action, for Griffin realized something that differentiated himself from the Shriekian. He saw innocence in the eggs and even though Griffin wanted so badly to hurt them, he could not bring himself to doing it. *It is not their fault they are being brought into this world and raised that way*, Griffin said to himself. He took one last look at the body of Shriekian eggs and then reluctantly swam off in the other direction of where his vision had led him.

Griffin had now exceeded his time in which he had previously practiced holding his breath, and he surely could feel it getting to him. The detour he took while discovering the Shriekian babies had taken a great deal of his time, and had he not stopped, he would be to the surface by now. His heart began to skip every other beat and his lungs and chest burned like a furnace at full force. *Two more turns!* he thought. Griffin took a left and made his way down the second to last waterway.

Now starting panic, Griffin kicked his legs quicker and pulled his arms through the water as fast as he could. He released a great deal of the remaining oxygen he had within him as his face turned from a bright red into a darkened purple. With his strides through the water shortening and a sharp pain passing through his skull from the lack of air, Griffin could see the last right turn up ahead. With all the lingering energy he could bring about, he lunged his body around the last right turn of the passageway. He could see light from above. It was the surface! The boy's drowsy blue eyes opened and closed as he convulsed in the water and gasped for air, inhaling water into his lungs.

Griffin was now but two feet from the water's surface. With once last kick of his fatigued legs, he broke the surface coughing and spewing the lake out of his lungs. Going in and out of consciousness, he slowly eased his body toward the shore. His limp head crashed in and out of the water as he fought the desire to give in. And just when Griffin thought he could no longer endure, he felt earth beneath his feet. He could touch the rock bottom and limped his body to the shore and flopped himself on the muddy ground with half his body still in the Shriekian Lake.

Continuing to cough up water, Griffin took in sharp shallow breaths. His body was going into shock. He lay on his back as his eyesight left him and returned back to him. Lifting up his quivering hand, he stuffed it into his right pocket and pulled out Snolan's whistle. Putting the piece to his mouth, he sent air through it with all the strength he could congregate. It sent a brief yet loud high-pitched sound throughout the air. Griffin's ghostly face then slumped into the soil, and all consciousness was gone from his being. And there the helpless boy rested at the shore of the Shriekian Lake.

Many precious minutes had passed when something emerged through the trees at a high velocity. It was Snolan, the castle guardian of the Critins and whom Griffin had called upon with the whistle. She had heard his call and had come to his aid. She flew through the forest at full force, her white scales gleaming in the sun and her powerful wings tearing through the air. Her eyes were wide with apprehension, and her heart so longing to find her lost friend it could be heard from across mountains and rivers. The boy was in her sight, and she hastily flew to the ground and landed on her all fours before him.

"Griffin!" she spoke intensely. "Griffin!" she said again, this time nudging him with her large nose. "I am here, Griffin. I am here...please." A tear dripped from her blue eyes and down her scaly cheekbone. The dragon knelt down by the motionless boy's side, placing her head on his chest. Even though it was very faint, Snolan could hear his heartbeat. Ever so carefully,

Snolan took up Griffin's clothing in her teeth in effort to carry him to the Critin castle.

As she did this, something hastily began to come out of the Shriekian lake. First, out of the lake rose two pointed tips that appeared to be towers. The Shriekian castle was emerging from the lake. Snolan's eyes widened at the sight of this and watched in utter shock. Moments later, the castle was fully out of the lake as the drawbridge collapsed. Snolan dragged Griffin's body until he was completely out of the lake. She then stood firmly in front of the boy, ready for what was to come, ready to fulfill her responsibility, and ready to protect.

THE SINGLE EGG

A pair of glowing red eyes could be seen in the darkness from inside the castle where the door had opened. Snolan lowered her head and braced herself. Her eyes stayed fixed on the silhouette that stood in the doorway. The creature that owned the pair of red eyes revealed itself as it stepped forward. It was Gotham. His eyes locked onto Snolan's as he grinned, showing off his razor-sharp teeth. Snolan's eyebrows lowered, giving her a menacing look.

"My good sister!" Gotham shouted to her from across the lake. "How have you been?" He cackled.

Snolan raised her head and powerfully replied, "You are *no* brother of mine. And you shall not have the courtesy of claiming me as your family." She took a step toward the water's edge, still keeping Griffin safely behind her.

"The last time I saw you, you were still *trying* to protect that feeble species. I see nothing has changed since then."

"The Critins are my family, and they are anything but weak. Go back down to your wretched swamp, and let us be!" Snolan roared from the lake's shore to where Gotham still stood in the doorway.

The dragon began to pump his wings up and down, causing wind to stir about. He pushed off from the doorway and became airborne, hovering in place above the Shriekian castle. "Come with me, Snolan! And together we shall share this throne!"

Snolan let out a deafening roar in disagreement.

"Then you shall perish with the rest of them. Now give me the boy, or I will take him from you." The dark dragon worked his large wings effortlessly as his four legs dangled beneath him.

"If you want him! Come and claim him!" Snolan then ran alongside the lakeshore gaining speed until she opened her wings and took flight directly toward Gotham.

"Then you have chosen death!" With a quick swipe of his wings, he drove his body forward. And the two dragons were hurling toward one another like two trains on a single track. Just before crashing into each other, Snolan let out a deadly inferno through her mouth. Gotham dodged the flames and began to fly straight up in the air. Snolan quickly changed her route and followed closely behind him. It was no question that Gotham was much larger than her and had a massive wingspan that allowed him to fly at a higher speed. But Snolan was a more efficient flyer and could maneuver quickly in any direction she desired.

Gotham shifted his head downward to see where Snolan was located as he led the two of them higher in the air. When he had about fifteen yards between himself and Snolan, he quickly let up his ascent and shifted his body around. He was nose-diving straight for Snolan!

The mighty dragon tucked his wings to the sides of him, making him more aerodynamic. Once again, the two feuding dragons were vertically heading straight toward one another. Just before the collision, Snolan swerved off to the right of Gotham and slashed his side with her sharp claws. He bellowed in pain, and just before Snolan was nearly out of his reach, he swung his tail toward her as she was passing. Gotham's spiked tail struck Snolan's left shoulder, greatly slicing it. This caused the rest of her body to spin out of control and toward the water below. Tumbling downward, she found her wings just as she was about to make an impact, and she grazed the water with her front legs.

Still lying off to the side of the lake in large blades of grass was Griffin, his head slouched to the side and his body soaked to the bone from escaping the Shriekian castle. Gotham and Snolan continued their airborne battle as Griffin's eyes started to widen. He was regaining consciousness. Griffin blinked and squinted until he was finally able to fully open his blue eyes. He carefully brought his chest upward, placing his hands beneath him. Disoriented, he observed his surroundings. Grasping that he was not inside his cement prison and now on dry land, the act of fleeing their castle was coming back to his memory. "I am out..." he gasped in disbelief.

Griffin then could hear the sound of a crackling fire. He looked around him and saw nothing of the sort. The boy then turned his head upward and could see huge balls of flame being exchanged by two airborne beings. "Sno-laaaaaaan!" he cried. Griffin tried to get up off the grass as he kept his eyes fixed on the two battling dragons. His body was too weak, and he could not bring himself to his feet. He slumped back down to the ground, horrified and helpless. Gotham was overpowering Snolan, and her wings had lacerations all about them and blood was trickling from her mouth as Gotham continued to pursue her.

Griffin looked about his surroundings once again, desperately seeking some kind of weapon he could assist Snolan with. "I need my shortbow!" he stated aloud. His eyes fell on the whistle that he used to call Snolan. Griffin then glanced to the lake and then to the golden whistle. *That looks a lot like the same whistle Sable used to call Golydon with.* he frantically thought. Taking the whistle up in his hand, he dragged his limp body over to the water's edge. He placed half the whistle into the lake and kept the other half exposed. Breathing the now precious air into his lungs, he sent a shrill sound throughout the water. "Golydon, we need you," the boy muttered. He looked to the Shriekian lake, and it was as still as could be.

Griffin could hear Snolan's weakening roars as Gotham continued to attempt to bring her out of the sky. Cupping his two hands around his mouth to amplify his voice, Griffin shouted once more, "*Snolaaaaaaan!*"

This time he was heard. And not only Snolan, but also Gotham heard him as well. The dark dragon promptly took his attention off Snolan and flew straight toward Griffin where he rested. Seeing Gotham's intentions, Snolan hastily soared over the dark dragon and landed directly in front of Griffin once more, prepared to defend.

"Snolan," Griffin began, "go get help! Go get the soldiers!"

She turned her lengthy neck around to see him, "I am not leaving you, Griffin!"

Gotham landed before her as she stood as a barrier between the boy and him. "Step aside, or I will do away with you right now, Snolan!" Gotham's sharp tail was dangling over the Shriekian lake off the shore as his feet dug into the mud.

"Griffin, run!" Snolan bellowed.

The boy struggled to his feet and crumpled to the ground once more and then tried to drag his body into the forest in front of him.

Unexpectedly, a large body of water began to spray up from across the lake. It was enormous and was disrupting the whole swamp, causing waves to thrash about and crash into the Shriekian castle that was still submerged. Gotham's back was turned to this large wave. He turned his neck around and boasted, "Ah, right on time!" He turned back to Snolan and

Griffin. "I command the Shriekian now! They heed *my* word and have come to return the boy to the Shriekian castle."

Griffin squinted his eyes and studied more intently at what was happening in the lake. He then exclaimed, "That is *no* Shriekian!" A moment after these words left his lips, an enormous water creature leapt half of its body out of the water and clasped its jaws around Gotham's tail that was hanging over the water's edge. The water beast had a long rubbery neck that nearly exceeded the whole length of its body. It owned four slick fins that allowed it to cut through water with ease. The shell on its back was exquisitely in the shape of a pentagon that gave it a turtle-like look.

Golydon had heard Griffin's call. Gotham snarled with anguish as the animal dragged him down into the water. The struggling dragon dug his claws into the ground as he was being pulled back into the deep muck. Gotham let out a final howl as the aquatic creature pulled him completely under. Nether Gotham or Golydon could be seen. All Snolan and

Griffin could witness were bubbles rising to the top of the lake where Golydon had taken him beneath.

"How did Golydon know to come, Griffin?" Snolan gasped.

Griffin did not say a word; instead he opened the palm of his hand, revealing the green, wooden whistle. "Of course! The whistle reacts differently in water!"

The two of them continued to scan the lake for any sign of their companion that had unquestionably saved their lives.

Griffin, who was still lying by the water's edge, expressed, "Where is Golydon, Snolan?" Placing his hands beneath him once more, Griffin's trembling legs finally found their footing. Snolan moved closer to him, allowing him to lean on her. The dragon's body was battered and bruised from the aerial battle she just endured. Griffin placed his arm on her side that was not wounded and used her as support. His eyes broadened with uneasiness and dismay as they saw no sign of their friend.

Bubbles started to rise to the middle of the water where the Shriekian castle towered. But coming to the surface was not Golydon. A black claw burst from the lake and clasped down on the drawbridge that was ajar. The being pulled itself up and out of the water into the doorway to the castle. It was Gotham. The dragon hacked up water out of its lungs and had gaping cuts where Golydon had attacked him. The beast glared back at Griffin and Snolan from across the lake and then made his way back into the castle. The drawbridge closed behind him, and the Shriekian domain began to sink back to the depths once more.

Once again, foam started to arise to the surface of the lake just off the shore facing Griffin and Snolan. First, bubbles rose, then a wave started to move their way. The body of water progressed slowly toward them as they watched in anticipation. Breaking the top of the water emerged a prehistoric face with worry in its eyes. It was Golydon. The water creature struggled to make it to the shoreline where the two of them stood. Golydon's long neck exposed itself as it moved closer. The fins of the beast pushed gently through the water in discomfort as he finally made its way to them. His stunning green shell was fully exposed as half its body rested on the sand with the other half still in the water.

Griffin and Snolan moved toward him, trying to comfort the suffering animal. "Snolan, we have to do something! What can we do?" Griffin limped over closer to Golydon and stood face to face with him. "You saved us, Golydon, you know that...you have to know this." Griffin held out his two hands as the water animal rested its rubbery head in the palm of them.

Golydon looked into Griffin's eyes, and the boy knew the being understood. He lifted his head off Griffin's hand as Golydon shoved something forward through the water. It used its fin in doing so and pushed a large matter onto the water's side where Griffin stood. It was a bright, multicolored egg the size of a large dinner plate. It had vibrant colors of blue, green, yellow, and purple swirled all around it.

It shimmered in the daylight as Griffin gazed at it in confusion.

"Golydon is leaving us, Griffin," Snolan sobbed.

Golydon's head then slumped to the ground as Griffin attempted to intercept it. He fell to his knees before the suffering beast. "No!" Griffin shouted. As short breaths were being taken in from the creature, they grew shallower with every moment that passed.

Snolan walked over to where Griffin knelt. "Griffin," she wept, "there can only be one of this species alive at a time. This is Golydon's single egg that we must now protect."

Moments later, the shallow breaths of the creature had subsided, and Griffin took up the colorful egg in his arms.

THE RETURN

As they flew over the treetops, Griffin kept the egg securely pressed up against his chest with one arm wrapped around it and the other on the back of Snolan's neck for support. The sickly boy fought to keep his eyes open for exhaustion was once again setting in. The dragon's body moved steadily through the air. Her white scales had been slashed by Gotham's mighty tail, and she had puncture wounds from where he had sunk his teeth.

"This is my fault," Griffin stated as he continuously replayed Golydon's death over in his mind like a night terror that became reality. "I called on her! I am the reason she had to fight Gotham!" He looked at the egg as a tear rolled down his scarred cheekbone.

"Griffin," she spoke softly, "you have saved us all by sacrificing yourself to them many months ago. You must understand this." The castle could now be seen up ahead as they continued their flight at a slow pace. "Golydon was a very dear friend of mine." She paused for a moment and struggled to get out her words. "Golydon's sacrifice will be known to all."

The morning sun revealed itself as they made it over the Critin village. Even though Griffin had just witnessed a horrific scene, he felt a warm and comforting sensation overwhelm his body as he saw the town below and the Critin castle up ahead.

"What's Snolan carrying?" A Critin resident gasped while she walked down the village pathway. Many other Critins gazed up at the sky, and others made their way out of their stone huts to see what all the commotion was about.

"The boy has returned! The boy has returned!" The Critin villagers embraced each other in their feathered arms and rejoiced in exhilaration as they flew over. Snolan's tired wings slowed down as she approached the castle that rested atop the many mountainous boulders. She planted her four feet to the cement with the two sizeable doors sitting before them. She knelt down, and the tired boy slid off her back. He placed his hand on Snolan once again, using her for support.

Then without warning, a great wind began to rustle about. Griffin turned his head around. As he did this, all the Critin villagers were flocking to the castle platform where Snolan and Griffin stood. "You are back!" they shouted. "You returned!" They landed before them and embraced Griffin and Snolan. Two of the villagers walked ahead of them, opening the castle doors. The others braced Snolan and Griffin, and they helped the two heroes limp inside.

"Do you hear that?" Sable stated. Mogol and himself were in one of the castle dormitories. They had been endlessly working, calculating and reworking plans that they could use to get Griffin back from the Shriekian. Little did they know Griffin had come back to them. There was an infinite chatter echoing throughout the castle.

"Sure do hear that, Sable," Mogol agreed. "Sounds like the whole village is in here!"

Sable and Mogol hurriedly left the room and made their way down the castle hallway in confusion. They passed the portraits of the royal family of the diamond that clung to the walls. They passed the dining room with the oval-shaped table where they had nearly every meal. And then Mogol and Sable saw them.

Standing just inside the doorway was the whole Critin village surrounding Snolan and Griffin. The Critins divided, allowing them to be seen.

Griffin slightly smiled as Sable's and Mogol's eyes fell upon him. He then stretched his arms to a villager, handing her Golydon's egg. She took the egg, and not a moment later, Griffin's knees buckled before him.

Kyrene, a villager standing near Griffin, intercepted the falling boy before hitting the ground. "The boy needs assistance!" Kyrene exclaimed.

Sable then rushed to his side as the Critin family took the boy to his chamber where they could nurse him back to health.

Back in the room, Griffin rested on his soft bed. Mogol and Sable stood by his side, and Lennah, one of the castle assistants, brought warm linen towels and sweet herbal soup for Griffin.

"Will someone please call on Adria and give her knowledge that the boy has returned?" Sable stated.

Mogol nodded his head and left the room to seek out Adria.

Griffin's body shuddered every so often. He was clammy and was doused in sweat as his chest moved gently up and down.

Adria, who had been out in the woods practicing religiously with her bow and arrow, saw Mogol flying down to her.

He landed by her side. "My dear Adria, the boy has returned."

She did not say a word as she dropped her bow where she stood and ran off in the direction of the castle. She ran to the side castle door that was at the basin of a large rock mound.

A moment later, bursting through the doorway was Adria. Her jaw dropped as her vibrant green eyes held dismay within them. Feeling tears evolving, she walked to the bedside where he lay. She knelt down by him and noticed his hand was greatly swollen. Taking his injured limb up in her hand, she spoke, "You're back... you got away from them..."

Eyes still shut, Griffin mumbled something vaguely, "Golydon...Snolan's hurt."

Sable placed his talon on Griffin's shoulder. "Snolan is just fine, brave boy. She is being tended to."

Adria looked to Sable and questioned, "And what of Golydon?" Sable did not speak, but instead, his face dropped with a troubled expression. "Sable! Answer me!"

"Adria...Golydon has given us...an egg."

And then Adria knew. She placed the other hand that was not holding Griffin over her two eyes and sobbed in her sorrow.

AWAKENING

Ever since Griffin had left with the Shriekian, Adria had forgotten to keep in mind her *own* health. She did not sleep most the nights he was gone, nor did she eat proper meals. Sable and Mogol had grown increasingly uneasy about Adria and tried to get her to comply. However, Adria insisted she was not in harm's way of becoming ill and was fixated on bringing Griffin home safely. To help take her mind off of the missing boy, she drew sketches of the land of Aranwea and of the beings that inhabited it. The girl had grown rather fond of drawing and had kept her pieces of art bound up in an old-fashioned-looking notebook that had a small rope to tie around it to keep it all together.

A few days passed by. Griffin slept most of the time. He took in nourishment that the castle nurse, Aberdeen, provided for him. He was the Critin village's finest nurse, constantly tending to Griffin at all hours of the day and night. This Critin had distinct black markings that started from atop his head that descended down the spine to the tip of his lion-like tail. Aberdeen was not the only one who took care of the boy. Since Griffin had come home, Adria endlessly sat at the boy's bedside, bringing him bowls of herbal soups and medicines to place on his lacerations.

Adria sat in a small wooden chair, with her elbow on her knee and her head resting on the palm of her hand, as Griffin began to awaken. It was the fourth day of his return, and Griffin had gone in and out of sleep, never fully awakening or entirely conscious. His eyes halfway open, he turned his head and saw Adria sound asleep. He lightly smiled at the sight of her and began to rub his fatigued blue eyes.

This was the first time in months that Griffin sensed some indication of energy, some feeling of life. He placed his hand beneath him and sat up in the bed. Griffin then leaned his back up against the wall for support. Looking over to the right of him, the boy saw a striking shirt made out of fresh white linen that had gold-colored trim around the collar of it and the sleeves. Underneath it was a new pair a woven pants. Using the tips of his fingers, he pulled on his discolored green t-shirt that he had spent many days in. The boy wrinkled his brow in thought of discontent. Not wanting to reunite with Adria looking like a foul sea monster himself, he quietly attempted to pull the brown bedding off of him. He gazed at Adria and hoped she would not awaken.

Stepping onto the flooring, he then snatched the fresh clothing up in his hands. Tiptoeing to the doorway, he placed his hand on the doorknob ever so gently and turned it. The door propped open, and as it was nearly enough space for him to get through, the ancient castle door let out a loud *creeeeeak*. Griffin sunk his head down to his shoulders and squinted his eyes in misfortune.

"Griffin?" came a voice from behind him. The boy turned his body hastily around to see Adria wide awake and staring at him. "You're up! You are well!" She sprang up from the chair and made her way toward him. She tossed her arms around him, resting her head precisely on his chest where Griffin had just noticed the discoloration of his shirt.

Griffin hesitantly put his arms around her and joked, "Can we have this discussion after I have cleaned up and put on some proper attire?"

She let go of him. "Griffin, you remember *exactly* how *I* looked when you found me lying in that cage at the Shriekian lake."

The rather-embarrassed boy remarked, "Really? I look *that* bad?" He chuckled a bit and then grabbed her arm, bringing her close to him once more.

Putting her arms around him again she stated, "Very funny, Griffin Dominic. You don't know how good it is to see you."

Embracing each other, he replied, "Trust me... I know."

Bringing her arms away from him, she spoke, "I'll let Sable and Mogol know you are awake. Go get cleaned up, and I will have Lennah cook you up something to eat for when you are done, okay?" Griffin nodded his head in agreement as his shaggy hair flowed in front of his eyeballs. "And we must do something about that hair." She retorted.

Griffin rolled his eyes at her and swiped away the pieces of hair that was disrupting his eyesight. "I'll see you in a bit, Adria." Griffin pushed through the castle door and made his way to the corridor where he could tidy up.

Adria gave the news to Lennah that Griffin had awakened. She was delighted and more than happy to make Griffin a magnificent meal.

"Lennah, where is Sable and Mogol?"

"I think they are atop the Oval, my dear child."

Adria then raced through the castle and made her way to the spiral staircase that would lead her to the top of the entire castle. Opening the doors to the Oval, Mogol and Sable turned to look at her. She was glowing and breathing very heavily from running around the castle.

"Adria, is everything in its right manner?"

"Yes." She speedily went to the two of them. "Griffin has awakened! He is getting cleaned up right now, and Lennah is preparing a meal for him as we speak."

Mogol elevated his brow and widened his eyes in excitement. "Fantastic!" he exclaimed.

Sable placed his right talon on her shoulder and replied, "That is wonderful news, my dear. We will be right down to see him."

"Okay!" She shifted her body in the other direction and made her way out of the Oval.

Sable turned his body toward Mogol, causing the red diamond that hung around his neck to swing to the other side of him. "I have not seen Adria this lively in months, Mogol. It is essential that she starts to once more look after her own health."

Mogol scratched the top of his feathered head and smiled. "Adria will be just fine now that Griffin is home. Now we must have a grand festival for Griffin's homecoming. What say you?"

"Agreed."

The two of them then made their way through the two wooden doors and off of the Oval.

Griffin felt refreshed as he washed the stench from the Shriekian swamp off of his body. He only wished he could wash away the horrid memories he had endured along with it. He had an uncountable amount of scars that covered his back and neck. Some of these slashes were still in the process of healing, which made it difficult for Griffin to wash.

Griffin slipped into his new attire and shook his head from left to right, shaking off the excess water. He ran his fingers through his now smooth and untangled hair and took in a deep breath. He closed his eyes and expressed, "I'm home."

GRIFFIN'S BOW

As the boy walked back through the castle and to his room, he gazed around it. Nothing had changed. The same stained-glass windows clung to the walls, along with the different paintings and pictures. Griffin passed by a particular picture through the hallway that led to his room. He had always admired this piece of artwork, and he stopped for a moment to enjoy being in its presence once again. This painting was of the brilliant wilderness of Aranwea. It showed bright green hills and a large forest off in the distance. There was a crystal-blue river that ran through the landscape and the sky owned fluffy white clouds that nearly looked realistic enough to touch.

Appreciating the painting for a moment longer, Griffin's nose began to tug him in the other direction. He could smell the aroma of seasoned herbs and nuts, along with the fresh steaming fish of Aranwea. The boy's stomach ached with hunger as he followed the fragrance down the rest of the hallway and back into his room. He found the food that he longed for and sat down at the table that was placed a few feet from his bed.

There was no one else present in the room. Griffin was happy for this because he was about to use anything but proper table manners. He took the spoon in hand and dipped it in the brown substance of herbs and seasonings. He pressed it to his lips, slurping the warm liquid. Again, Griffin quickly plunged the spoon back into the wooden bowl and slurped it immediately. Setting the spoon to the side, he said aloud, "Oh, what the heck!" Taking it up in his hands the starving boy brought the whole bowl to his mouth and consumed the soup within seconds. Griffin then fed on the turquoise fish that was cooked to perfection and the many different berries and nuts that were near it.

As he was finishing up his much-needed meal, Griffin heard a knock on the door that was half open. "Come in!" he mumbled with his mouth still occupied.

Sable pushed the rest of the door open and stepped inside, and Mogol trailed closely behind him. Griffin quickly swallowed the remainder of food in his mouth and stood up out of the chair.

"Please, Griffin. Sit and rest." Sable walked to him, his talons clicking as he did so.

"Sable...Mogol...it's great to see you," the boy expressed.

Sable opened his golden brown arms and embraced Griffin. The boy wrapped his arms around the diamond bearer. Sable spoke, "Griffin Dominic, seeing you back in the Critin castle brings me remembrance of our salvation, but it is more than that." He paused and let go of the boy, looking at Griffin with his yellow cat-like eyes. "It is more than that because you are beyond just our source of freedom...

you are our family. It is great to have you back, my boy."

Mogol walked toward Griffin and placed his left talon on Griffin's shoulder, "Things just have not been in order without you."

The boy's smile slowly faded from his face as he turned away from the two beings and strolled over to his bed. The soft cushion sank down as he sat, and when he did Griffin had a confused expression about his face. Looking to the ground, he clasped his hands together and placed them on his lap. Still gazing at anything but Sable and Mogol, Griffin delayed for a moment then asked, "Did you *try* to find me?" Griffin's voice was deep and solemn. He glanced up. "I mean, at all?" His blue eyes were a bit watery and shimmered in the reflection of the candles that was illuminating the undersized room. His face was hopeful as the anxious boy waited their response.

"Griffin, of course, we did!" Mogol stepped to the side of Sable, getting into better view. The Critin's mouth was agape, and his beak was tilted toward the ground, which caused his two horns to sprout from his head aiming at the ceiling. "My boy..." He moved even closer to Griffin standing a few feet before him. "The Shriekian castle did not rise up!" He motioned his two talons to the roof as he spoke passionately. "We sent our soldiers to the Shriekian lake. We drove arrows upon arrows into their murky depths in hopes to surface them!"

"Because that is what we did when we attacked them at the lake many months ago," Griffin said, trying to understand all that Mogol was saying to him.

"Precisely." Sable stepped closer to Griffin as well. "Griffin, the Shriekian domain would not rise." The Critin placed his hand on his chest where his beating heart rested beneath. "They would not surface the castle for they *knew* we would be coming for you. The army went to the swamp every morning, midday, and evening since you had left, Griffin." Sable paused and found his words once more. "Griffin, you have saved our kind. My boy, you have shown the ultimate act of bravery that I have not witnessed ever in my days until now."

The door creaked open behind him. The three of them turned to see Adria peering her head around the corner into the room. "Sorry, I don't mean to be interrupting, but there is someone here to see you, Griffin." Adria pushed her long brown hair out of her eyes and tucked it behind her ear as she eagerly opened the remainder of the door. Standing behind her was a small being. It wrapped its little arms around Adria's left leg as it peeked around, looking at Griffin.

"Polco!" Griffin announced as he motioned the youngster over to him.

Polco's round feathered cheeks lifted, and his large turquoise eyes brightened as he toddled over to Griffin. Griffin stood up and knelt down by the small Critin. Polco shyly stuttered, "H...how are you, sir?" The Critin held something in his right talon.

Griffin smiled greatly and put his hand atop Polco's feathered head. The youngster had just begun to grow his set of horns and had two undersized stubs sprouting. Griffin replied, "I am *much* better now that I am back with you and everyone else, Polco." The small Critin beamed at Griffin as if he were in the presence of some sort of deity. "Do you have something for me, Polco?"

Nodding his head up and down, Polco presented Griffin with his shortbow. Before Griffin had left with the Shriekian, he gave Polco his beloved shortbow to watch over while he was gone. The bow was in just as beautiful condition just as Griffin left it. The gold trim about the sides was shiny and untouched and the words *"Steady Eye and Fire"* were still perfectly engraved in the wooden part of it. The stringing was still sturdy and strong as Griffin took it up in his hand.

Examining it for a moment, the boy spoke, "Looks like you have taken great care of it. Thank you, Polco."

Without a moment's hesitation, the starstruck youngster wrapped his arms around Griffin's neck as the boy knelt before him. The boy chuckled then took his right arm and enclosed it around Polco and his petite wings, bringing him close to him.

Polco let go of Griffin's neck and said, "I have to get back home, but please come visit my hut, Mr. Griffin."

"You can count on it." Griffin grinned.

THE BURNS

Sable then took the little one by his talon and walked him out of the room. Mogol followed them as they left.

"Looks like you got a little fan there, Griffin," Adria joked. She assembled herself at the table's chair, and Griffin sat back on his bed with his shortbow securely in his hand. Griffin gazed at the bow he had just been reunited with. "How are you feeling, Griffin?"

Finally taking his attention off the bow, he looked to her and spoke, "Oh just fine. I'll be ready to start training the army in the morning."

Adria squinted her eyes and crossed her arms in disapproval. "Griffin, you need to rest for many days now. I know what it is like to be with them...I know what you went through."

"Adria, I am fine. We need to start training as..."

"Griffin!" She interrupted. "You have been bedridden for many days now. Please just rest for a while..."

The boy let out a large sigh and slouched back on his bed placing his two hands beneath his head. "You are right."

"Thank you," she replied. Griffin then took his throbbing hand up in his other one and began to massage it. "What happened to your hand, Griffin? It is as big as a balloon. Lennah is working on fashioning you some sort of cast out of tree bark."

Griffin started to recall the many days spent with the Shriekian, living in their hatred and vile surroundings. He remembered one night spent with them that would haunt him for the rest of his days. He began, "I knew it was going to be bad, Adria." He turned his face so he could see her.

Adria's eyes were locked onto his as she awaited his next words. Her heart was moving quickly in her chest causing the hair on the back of her neck to stand on edge. She knew of the torture Griffin was about to speak of, but she sat and anticipated his next words nonetheless.

"The Shriekian treated me just like I expected them to. They would visit me daily, bringing me scraps of something or other just to keep me alive. Many times, they would come in the prison, sometimes bringing many of them. And"—Griffin stopped for a moment—"and they would take turns slashing me with their claws, cackling at me like I was some kind of abused animal. Well...I guess that is exactly what I was. An abused creature left to torture for their enjoyment." Griffin covered his now-watering eyes.

"Griffin, its okay." Adria walked over and sat by his bedside. She took his hands away from his cowering face. The boy would not look at her.

He released a mouthful of air. "But one night, it was different, Adria."

She pulled her face back in nervousness. "What do you mean?"

"One night...they took me from my room. It was about one month from being held captive there, and I had kept track of the days the best I could. This was one of the first nights where I actually found a bit of sleep. I was awoken by the door to my prison being opened, and before I could react I was being dragged by both of my arms through the hallway. The Shriekian took me to a large room. That is where I saw Gotham for the first time..."

Griffin continued to tell Adria of the horrid encounter he had with them. This was nothing like any torture Griffin had endured being with the Shriekian. Ever since that night, Griffin had never fully recovered.

"Gotham continued to question me where I was from and if there was another world. I tried to convince him that you and I were one of a kind. Just like him and Snolan. I tried to tell him there was no other world and that all other humans had gone missing, just like the dragons." Adria used her hand to move Griffin's shaggy hair out of his watering eyes. "But...he did not believe me. Gotham was somehow convinced that another land did exist and wished to take it over as well."

Adria continued to sit at his bedside and took in the words Griffin was revealing to her. She softly asked, "But, Griffin, the Shriekian believed that you were under their control, right?"

"Yes."

"Then why would they not have faith in what you were saying?"

"I know the Shriekian *did* believe me, but... Gotham was different. He is smarter than they, and even though he thought I was under their control, Gotham still thought I came from another place." Griffin paused again, struggling to articulate his next words. A tear trickled down his scarred cheek as he quickly whisked it away with his white linen sleeve. "So...they started to drag me off to the side of the large room..." His voice was trembling with force. "And there I stood before a pool of water that was set in the ground of the castle. The body of water was not wide, but it appeared to be deep. It was a watery hole...a dark black abyss. And in that pool of water were...were hundreds upon hundreds of eels...electric eels."

Adria clasped her hand across her mouth in dismay. She looked at Griffin and knew what his next words would be. Her heart pounded even faster as she lightly shook her head from left to right. "No..." She wept.

"Yes..." Griffin stated as his blue vibrant eyes filled with tears. "When I would not agree with Gotham that there was another world...they pushed me into that pool of water." Griffin sat up and slid off his bed. He walked to the other side of the room with his hands on his hips and his back turned to Adria. "I could feel each and every pulse of electricity being sent throughout my body, Adria..." He turned to her and pulled on the sleeve to his shirt, revealing his forearm. "These are not bite marks, Adria, nor are they claw marks...these are burns from the eel's stingers." The markings that Griffin had on his arms were welted and scarred, and his limbs were not the only parts of his body that was damaged. Griffin's back, neck, stomach, and legs were also consumed with scorching that the eels left him to endure with.

Adria did not know what she could possibly say to comfort the boy. She had lived with the Shriekian, or more of underwent the anguish they put her through when they captured her nearly two years ago. But Adria never went through the torture that Griffin spoke of. "I...I cannot fathom that, Griffin." She got up and walked toward him. The boy slid his sleeves back down his forearms, covering up his disfigurements. "You are much stronger than I, Griffin." He looked to the ground, not making eye contact with her. "I could not take their torture, or their temptation. You have overcome both of these things." She settled her right hand upon Griffin's cheek. "Look at me, Griffin." Keeping his face downward, he lifted his blue eyes. Adria paused momentarily. "These scars that you have...they are beautiful for they represent your loyalty, your bravery, and the love you have for us. They are nothing to be ashamed of, Griffin."

Griffin once again turned his face away from her. He waited for a moment and tried to understand what Adria was telling him. *How could these be beautiful?* The boy thought. "I...I just don't want to tell anyone about them for a while, okay, Adria?"

She nodded her head in agreement and stated, "You have my word."

Five weeks passed and Griffin began to get his strength back. The boy was lively for the first time in months and felt like he was getting back to his normal self. Adria would still not keep him out of her sight. She took care of Griffin throughout his recovery, despite the issue that Griffin thought he did not need her to. No matter how hard the boy tried, Adria would not leave his side until he was fully recovered.

Griffin and Snolan sat beneath a gigantic redwood tree just off to the side of the Critin village. The boy rested in the blades of grass with his hands under his head. He gazed up at the infinite branches of the redwood tree and said, "Snolan?"

"Yes, Griffin?" The mighty dragon lay next to Griffin with her chin resting on her front two legs. The dragon still had imprints on her neck where Gotham had sunk his teeth and lashed his tail out to her. And even though she still had some markings, Snolan had made a full recovery from the incident at the Shriekian lake.

Griffin sat up and placed his hands behind him for support. "I don't know how to figure out this riddle, Snolan." Griffin scratched his head and brushed his long locks back. "'You must not let it glow?' I just don't understand."

Snolan let out air through her enlarged nostrils and raised her head up. The dragon's prestigious horns were sharp and were jutting back from her white scaly head. Snolan's deep blue eyes directed themselves toward Griffin. "Eden also told you that the riddle will come to you in your most desperate time of need, is this truth?"

"Yes, Snolan." Griffin placed his right hand atop her nose and patted it lightly. He chuckled a bit. "That is what I am worried about! How much more desperate does it have to get?"

Snolan grinned, revealing her jagged teeth.

"*Heyyyyyy!*" came a voice flying over them. Mogol planted his two talons to the soil under the redwood. "Good day, my dear friends!" He rustled his golden wings about, causing feathers to float to the ground. "Being *exceptionally* lazy today, I see." Mogol laughed. Griffin and Snolan looked to each other and rolled their eyes. "Well, the festival celebration starts in nearly an hour! You two are the main events, and you do not wish to be looking like a bunch of underdressed brutes, now do you?"

Griffin stood up and brushed a leaf off of his long-sleeved linen. Griffin walked toward Mogol and teased, "Of course not, Mogol. Now you did keep my clothes that I had worn when I was with the Shriekian." Griffin turned his head back to Snolan and sent a wink her way. "I wish to wear those!"

"Very funny, my boy." Mogol scowled at him as Snolan attempted to hold her laughter back. "Your proper attire is awaiting you in your dormitory." Mogol peeked his feathered head around to see Snolan. "And as for you, Snolan. Lennah has prepared a magnificent wardrobe for you." Mogol spread his wings out, ready to take flight once more. "We shall meet at the basin of the castle boulders in one hour. Until then, my good comrades!" Mogol motioned his wings up and down freely and took flight toward the Critin Castle.

THE CELEBRATION

Griffin nearly finished getting ready for the festivities when Sable knocked on the door to his room. "Come in!" Griffin hollered. He was buttoning up a black woven shirt. The top he wore was stunning and had a white collar and white cuffs at the bottom of the sleeves. At the base of the shirt there was red beads and golden feathers that were strung to the sides of it. Griffin also wore a pair of slick black pants and white moccasins to go with it. The boy had also just received a suitable haircut, and no longer had his stringy hair flopping in his face, preventing his vibrant blue eyes to be seen.

Sable pushed the door open to his room. The Critin looked at the boy from head to toe and stated, "Looking very fetching, Griffin, very fetching indeed."

Griffin chuckled a bit and replied, "Ha, yeah, I can't remember the last time I dressed this nice." Griffin finished buttoning up his shirt. "Are we almost ready?"

Sable walked closer to him, his talons clacking on the hard surface. "Yes, yes we are nearly ready." Sable delayed for an instant. "I...I wanted to give you something." He held out his hand to Griffin. There was a bronze chain dangling from his talons. It was a necklace. And on the band was a golden feather at the end of it. "It was...Vector's chain, Griffin. My son's."

Griffin's blue eyes widened as he gazed at the necklace and then back to Sable. Doing another double take, the boy asked, "Sable...are you sure?"

"Yes, Griffin." The being smiled. "If you would desire it, I want you to have it."

Griffin took the chain up in his hand and studied it intently.

"Thank you, Sable. This means a lot. A whole lot."

Sable tussled Griffin's hair about with his talon. "We will be starting shortly. Do not be late!" He then exited the room. Griffin placed the chain around his neck and clipped it securely around the back. It hung perfectly about his collar with the golden feather placed on the center of his chest.

The festival was a mass celebration of all Critins. Old and young Critin villagers had all come together to honor Griffin's homecoming. Stone huts that the villagers dwelled in sat along each side of the pathway that led down the Critin Village. Each of these stone huts was not their normal gray tint, but instead, they contained decorations about them. The small houses each had multicolored banners hanging about them, flowing in early summer air. The creatures all waited patiently for the boy and Snolan to make their appearance. Each Critin also had new attire about them. Many of them sported shiny vests that slipped flawlessly around their feathered wings and arms. Others had painted the tips of their wings in shades of red, green, and blue. And at the end of the long pathway through the township was a massive round table made out of the redwood trees that inhabited the Rogon Woods. The village was lively and joyous as music from a flute was being played. The Critin family conversed with one another as they waited for their main event.

Adria was also in the Critin village, anticipating the festivities to begin. She sat and chuckled with two Critins. Adria was wearing an exquisite white dress that had golden feathers draping down from the bottom. The dress exceeded well past her knees and had a gold ribbon that tied around her waste, allowing the dress to flow perfectly. The threads that held the dress together made a lovely golden design. Her hair was wavy and ran down the sides of her rounded face past her shoulders.

Griffin awaited Snolan's presence atop the oval. He could hear the unbroken chatter from down below the castle where all expected his company. *Why am I nervous?* the boy asked himself. Griffin was excited for the celebration, but he couldn't help but feel a bit intimidated that all had come together to see him. He thought back to his first days in Aranwea. He recalled the many feuds he had with the Critins. Griffin touched his scarred cheek and thought back to when Vetch (one of the army leaders) had thrust his talon across Griffin's cheek, leaving imprints. Griffin smiled and was proud of how far he had come with them. He took pride in how he helped this once suffering race become prosperous once again.

"Your ride is here, Master Griffin." Startled, Griffin turned around to see Snolan touching down to the cool cement castle top.

Griffin rolled his eyes. "Snolan, please never refer to me as Master Griffin."

Snolan smirked and knelt down so he could climb up on her back. The dragon was wearing a silver vest that was made to fit around her wings, chest, and front legs. It was beaded, and it shimmered in the sunlight, reflecting off of her white scales. As they plummeted to the ground, the once restless town died down and watched intently. Landing at the basin of the castle, Snolan and Griffin made their way down the castle pathway. The whole village lined up on either side of the castle cheering and chanting Griffin's name. Griffin blushed as he continued down the path. He looked to Snolan and chuckled a bit as she did the same.

Bursting through the crowd of feathered beings was a group of little Critins. These youngsters were considered children in the Critin community, and all ran up to Griffin pouncing on him. They tugged at his arms as Griffin knelt down to their level and allowed them to wrap their feathered arms around him. The little ones ran back off into the crowd as Griffin and Snolan made their way down the path. They were nearly to the end when Griffin asked, "Hey, Snolan do you see Adria? I have been keeping an eye out for her and I don't see her anywhere."

Snolan glanced to the wondering boy and replied, "She is here, Griffin. Do not fret."

"I...I mean I am not worrying about it. I just don't want her to miss out on our celebration is all."

Sable stood at the end of the pathway as the two of them approached him. He placed his talon in the air, asking for silence to set in. Snolan walked to the right side of the pathway. Sable placed his talon that was in the air on Griffin's shoulder. "My Critin family!" Sable shouted so all could hear. "This boy has returned!"

All Critins raised their talon in the air and cheered in joy. When the noise had subsided, Sable declared, "Today...we celebrate! We rejoice for the homecoming of Griffin and the safety of Snolan. We rejoice for our brilliant future that is in store for us." Sable paused for a moment. "I know that there is evil that still lingers in Aranwea. But this evening, we count our many blessing that we have been given. Let us make this a night to remember!"

The hundreds of Critins cheered as Griffin stood and watched in amazement. His cheeks were red as he grinned. The pathway soon became filled with moving bodies as Griffin looked off to the side. He saw Adria standing there with her eyes on him. Walking away from Sable, he went to her. The boy nervously stated, "I...I didn't see you in the crowd earlier." He rubbed the back of his neck with his hand. "By the way"—he rushed his next words—"you look great."

The girl's face flushed with redness. She said, "Well, you don't look all that bad yourself." Adria then brushed her right hand atop Griffin's head. "I see you finally got a haircut." She chuckled a bit and started to move away from him. Turning back, she teased, "It's nice to see your eyes for once."

Griffin followed her as they made their way to the large redwood table where the feast awaited them. This was no ordinary meal that was typically served in Aranwea. This spread was much more than that. The table was overflowing with plates and platters of an assortment of foods. The Critins of Aranwea had gone through great lengths searching all over the land to find rare and diverse fare that could be enjoyed by all. There were dishes upon dishes of fresh rice with vegetables and herbs. Another side of the table had large bowls made of wood flourishing with nearly every kind of fruit. And the fish of Aranwea that was served was not its normal turquoise tint. But instead this main dish had seasonings atop it that were newly harvested from the Rogon woods. The supper was lively as the whole Critin village conversed as one complete family.

After the meal had ended, all Critins joined in the middle of the Critin village to continue the celebration. A group of twenty Critins brought out their finest instruments and started to play an upbeat tune. Many of them had flute-like tools; others had small pieces of metal that they would cling together to make different-pitched sounds. And one Critin had beneath her circular tubes of lumber that she hit across with a large piece of wood to create a deeper sound. The song they played was joyous and could make one feel as though not a worry existed in their life. It caused a sort of curious sensation about the village that only brought smiles and merriment.

Griffin sat off to the side on a smoothed tree stump and watched the active village. He thought back many weeks ago when he was in utter grief living with the Shriekian. *Now look where I am. I'm home*, he pondered. The boy continued to watch the beings as they started to now dance to the music that was being played. They hopped along to the fast beat, linking arms with one another and spreading their wings out wide. Others flew above them and twirled in the air, like airplanes performing skywriting. Griffin was clapping his hands to the song's sweet tune and tapping his foot when a hand presented itself before his face. Griffin gazed up and saw Adria standing before him. "Come on!" she stated with a contagious smile.

Realizing her intentions, the boy waved his hands in front of himself timidly stating, "No... no...no, Adria. I'm not dancing."

She placed her hand upon her hips and pouted in disappointment. "Griffin Dominic can save a whole kind, but he cannot dance?" She then leaned over and grabbed his wrist. "I find *that* hard to believe." Adria yanked on Griffin's arm as he rose to his feet. He followed her out to the area where the rest of the dancing Critins resided.

"Adria!" Griffin whined. "I really don't want—"

"Shhhhhh!" she interrupted. "Just listen to the music and follow my steps." Griffin rolled his eyes and placed his right hand around her waist as she set her hand upon his arm. Adria and Griffin clasped their other hands together, slightly raising them and then began to move back and forth to the beat. "See, Griffin? Its not *that* bad."

The boy had a smug look on his face as he took a step back from her and twirled her slowly around with his right hand. Bringing her closer to him once again, Adria stared at Griffin, being pleasantly surprised. They continued to sway in sync. They were the reflecting sunlight moving along with the calming ocean. Griffin released his hand from her waist once again as she spun away from him until their arms locked. He gave a quick tug and brought her near him once more. Griffin boasted, "I said I didn't want to dance, not that I didn't know how." Adria was the one who was now rolling her eyes in irony as they continued to dance for many of the following songs.

Mogol and Sable watched the festival off to the side. Mogol saw Griffin and Adria dancing in the middle with the villagers around them also taking part. The two of them sat in wooden chairs with a large mug of fresh springwater in their hands. Mogol nudged Sable with his feathered elbow. Catching the diamond bearer's attention, he then tipped his head toward the two of them dancing. Mogol voiced, "Griffin and Adria are getting along particularly well, wouldn't you say, sir?" Sable smiled at the sight of them enjoying each other's company. "The boy must not get distracted." Mogol insisted. "It is essential that the Shriekians' weakness is revealed. And Griffin is the only one of us who can succeed in doing so."

Sable placed the wooden mug up to his beak. Using his forked tongue, he consumed the cool liquid. Taking it away from his mouth, he spoke, "And, my dear friend, what Adria and Griffin have will only aid them in what is going on in this land. After so much suffering they have both endured, they need joy in their lives. You must see it cannot be done with just Griffin or solely Adria. It must be both." Sable then took the red diamond in his hand. "This is safe." He showed the gem to Mogol. "That is what is important right now."

MOLIDON

A few days passed since the mighty celebration, and the whole town seemed to still be buzzing. The gathering was a much-needed occasion that allowed the Critins to realize and remember the many blessings they still had even though they were at war. It endorsed the fact that no matter what was taking place, no matter the struggles they were enduring, they still had their Critin family. And in doing so, it also was a reminder of how they had to fight for this family to exist.

It was nearly noon when Mogol and Griffin strolled down the village's path to the large pasture that lay beyond. Griffin was going to be working with the Critin army for the first time since he had been back. The anxious boy held the shortbow in his right hand and had his quiver filled with arrows on his back. Practically bouncing up and down in eagerness, Griffin exclaimed, "I wonder how much they have improved! Are they a lot better since I left? By the way, who was it that you said trained them while I was away?"

Mogol walked along side the excited boy and answered, "Well, besides Vetch, of course, the others are Carlzar and Schmight. And I must say that they have done a fine job, a very fine job indeed." Mogol kicked a rock to the side with his foot and looked to Griffin. "I think you'll be quite impressed with their progress, my boy."

Griffin gripped his bow a bit tighter and sped up. "Well, let's get going, Mogol!" Mogol chuckled to himself as he hurried along to match Griffin's pace.

As they reached the top of the hill, they looked below and saw three hundred Critin soldiers. "Mogol..." Griffin gasped. He was spellbound, awestricken, and could not comprehend how many soldiers had now joined the army.

Mogol placed his talon on Griffin's right shoulder and, with a proud smile, spoke, "Since you left, Griffin, over two hundred soldiers merged." His cat eyes shifted toward Griffin, who was still mesmerized by the scene, mouth agape and body frozen. "They wanted to honor you for the sacrifice you made."

Griffin's heart raced with gladness and looked back toward Mogol. "Well, the Shriekian do not know *what* is coming to them!" Griffin then bounded down the steep, grassy slope and stopped himself before the two Critins who were leading them in their daily routine. The boy approached them as Mogol caught up to him.

The army leaders turned around to face them. "Hello," one of them greeted. "My name is Carlzar. I do not recollect a memory of us properly meeting, Griffin." The being was a bit shorter than the rest and owned light-green eyes the shade of the summer's lively hills.

The boy answered, "It's great to meet you!" Griffin glanced at Mogol. "I hear you both have been doing a fine job training the army!"

Carlzar modestly countered, "It was all them, Griffin. They have been putting in the hours out here."

"Well...it couldn't be done without either of you, of course," Griffin stated.

"Indeed," Mogol added.

The other army leader seemed to withhold some shyness as she took a step forward. "And...I'm Schmight. It is brilliant to make your proper acquaintance as well." This Critin was taller than the other and had a large pair of horns that admitted a reddish tint to them. Schmight had distinct small dots upon her face that made her unique from the rest.

Griffin swept his hand in front of his body and replied, "Pleased to make yours!" The two beings were warm and openhearted with Griffin. They each had done a magnificent job training the soldiers no matter how humbly they portrayed themselves.

After Griffin had conversed with the two of them, learning all about what they had been teaching the army and which groups of Critins were the most advanced, they got to work. Griffin adored being back with the soldiers, showing and teaching the ways of the bow and making bounds along the way. The boy could still not believe how many Critins had joined. Griffin still didn't grasp that the sacrifice he made many months ago had sparked a fire of encouragement in the villagers.

Griffin wandered to the other side of the pasture where a large group of soldiers were being directed. Wooden posts of all shapes and sizes rose from the grounds, with targets among them. Some of these targets had arrows protruding from them from previous practice. Each Critin was working intently, with their talons resting on the bow's string, arranged to set free each piercing arrow.

"Well, well, well." Griffin strolled down the large hill, causing him to gain a little speed. He stopped himself before a large Critin who had his back turned toward him. "If it isn't, Vetch."

Griffin crossed his arms smugly as the wind tugged on his gray t-shirt.

The last army leader faced the boy. Immediately, the utmost serious expression the creature resembled slowly diminished into a gradual smile. The being cocked his head to one side and shouted, "Five-minute break!" He strolled to Griffin, his chest held high. "I was wondering when I would be able to greet you again, my boy." He tussled Griffin's hair to the side with his talon. "You've been recovering for some time now, and you had plenty of company at the celebration." Vetch winked at Griffin with his cat eyes.

Griffin let out a sigh of slight annoyance then stated, "Well, if I do recall correctly you would not know what its *entirely* like being with the Shriekian, now would you, Vetch?"

"Oh here we go!" Vetch swayed his eyes and held back his cheekbones from grinning.

"Exactly!" Griffin made a soft fist and playfully hit Vetch's right shoulder. "You wouldn't know because *I* saved *your* life."

"You know you're much more feisty these days, Griffin." Vetch lowered his head to Griffin's level. His two horns were as black as the starless night and his eyes a deepened red, with a large scar passing through the right one. "Yes, Griffin you did save me."

A shadow passed over their heads, catching their attention. It was Sable moving quickly toward them, shouting, "The egg!" He got a bit closer. "Golydon's egg is hatching!" Sable circled around Vetch and Griffin. "Follow me!" As the diamond bearer glided through the air, Griffin ran swiftly beneath him. Over the hills the army was training on, Sable led the boy up to the Rogon woods before making contact with the ground once again. Stopping before the forest's entrance as well, Griffin placed his hands upon his knees, slouching over trying to regain his lost breath.

They entered the Rogon woods. The redwood trees that resided in the forest had large branches blocking out nearly all sunlight. They followed a small trail that led them to the stream that flowed from the Shriekian domain through the Critin village. Sable pushed through a sticky shrub that left yellow pollination about his golden feathers and motioned Griffin to follow. On the other side of the brush sat an undersized pool of water where the stream linked together. And in that stream lay the multicolored egg, completely cracked open and floating in the water. Along with Snolan and Adria, a few villagers had come to witness the birth of Golydon's baby. Adria walked closer to the water's edge and crouched down.

Griffin's eyebrows joined closer together in confusion as he wondered aloud, "Where is the baby?"

Adria scowled at Griffin and silently pressed her pointer finger to her soft lips. She then stuck her hand out over the water's surface. All were watching in silent intent as not a movement passed over them. Bubbles started to rise to the top where Adria held out her hand. And then breaking the surface, first came a small rubbery snout, followed by two gentle indigo eyes. Keeping the palm of her hand open, Adria glanced to the others witnessing the scene, mouth agape and face glowing in exhilaration.

The baby raised its long neck and moved through the water, closing the distance between Adria's hand. The pentagonal shell of the creature could now be seen just above the water. It was three feet in length and had distinct markings embedded in the shell with the shades of the multicolored egg it had just emerged from. The creature stopped beneath Adria's outstretched palm as it gazed upward and tilted its petite face to one side. Adria lowered her hand to the newborn's level as the baby pressed its smooth head up against her. Again, in utter amazement, she looked up to all those who were watching. Snolan moved cautiously over to Adria's side. The creature seemed to be accepting and taking in the attention. Adria was smiling, for the baby was now lightly slapping its front flippers in and out of the small pool, causing water to spray about. Snolan knelt down and extended her lengthy neck out. The creature curiously moved closer to her. "Hello, little one," Snolan spoke. Letting out a high-pitched screech, the baby began to rub its head against Snolan's cheekbone. "You look like Molidon to me."

HELP FROM THE HUMAN WORLD

A few weeks passed since Molidon was born. The youngster was growing at an extreme rate and grew a foot in length as each week passed. Once again, Adria was the one who was taking the most care of the new creature. In her mind, she told herself that she owed it to Golydon to see that the baby was well looked after. Adria would spend hours with the animal each day, checking on it and making sure it was safe. Molidon had grown exceedingly affectionate toward her and purred and yelped with gladness every time Adria came to greet it. Griffin too would help Adria with the new member whenever he had a chance, but it was challenging for the boy to find time since he was now healthy and the army needed him back for training.

It was early in the cool morning, as Adria awakened. Adria did not feel like herself. In fact, she had not been feeling well for some time now; however, she did not voice this. Her eyes were red and felt swollen. Even though Adria had been getting many hours of rest at night, she experienced a sense of unusual fatigue. She rubbed her hands up and down her pale arms that had goose bumps on them. As Adria made her way to the castle's kitchen area to find some breakfast, she found Sable.

"Good morning, Miss Adria!" Sable's mouth was half full of some kind of food as he greeted her.

She was looking at the ground as she gradually tilted her head upward, revealing the discomfort in her face. Her skin was as bland and pale, and her eyes drooped with involuntary ache. "Sable?" Her breath was short and shallow. "I do not feel well today."

Immediately Sable rushed over to her, nearly knocking over one of the kitchen chairs in his pursuit. Adria buried her face in her hands as Sable wrapped his arm around her and moved her closer to a nearby seat. Sitting down, she took her hands away from her hurting head.

"Adria?" Sable's voice was soft. "What is going on? How long have you been in this discomfort?" He squatted down to her eye level.

She gazed at the diamond bearer in dismay. "I...well I think this has been coming on for some time now, but I was hoping it would just go away." She sighed and placed her fingers on her throat. "I'm sick, Sable."

Sable rose to his feet as he demanded, "Well this will not do. Will not do at all." He started to move in the other direction. "I am going to find, Lennah. She will have—"

"Wait!" Adria cried. "Sable, I am concerned she cannot do anything." Adria swallowed a bit of saliva down setting fire to her esophagus. "I have felt this way before. I think I have am getting pneumonia."

He turned to face her once more. "Pneumonia?"

She nodded her head. "Yes, I had it when I was younger and was in the hospital for over a week." She paused. "It can only be treated with an antibiotic."

"What is this 'antibiotic' that you speak of, my dear?"

Adria began to cough profusely, clasping her hand around her sore throat. Sable winced in apprehension as he witnessed Adria struggling. When the coughing had subsided, she got the words out. "It is a medicine that cannot be found here. It can only be found in the human world."

Sable then crossed his feathered arms and gazed at the ground in contemplation. "Adria, there *has* to be a solution that we can request here in Aranwea."

She tossed her head from left to right. "Sable, you know our medication here is much different than in the human world."

The diamond bearer moved toward her once more, placing his talon upon her shoulder. He sent her an uneasy smile and reassured, "If this is what you need, my dear, it shall be done. Let me go seek out Griffin."

Adria nodded her head as she fought back her tears. *This is going to set us back so much*, she thought to herself. Adria was devastated and felt very shameful that someone had to go to the human world just for her. And even though she wished she could just endure the sickness until it finally went away, Adria knew that this was not an illness that you could just ignore forever for if gone untreated, the pneumonia could lead to death.

Sable roused Griffin from his morning slumber and explained to him all that was taking place. He told Griffin that a trip to the human world was in order and must be done as soon as possible. "I'd do it myself, but you know this is not possible, Griffin." Sable spoke.

"Where is, Adria?" Griffin insisted. Sable led him through the castle and up to the kitchen area where Sable had left her. Adria was still sitting in the chair with her hands covering her face. Her body was cool and clammy, but she did not feel the least bit cold for fever was setting in. As the boy spotted her, concern engulfed his system, causing his heart to jolt.

He went to her with haste and slowly knelt down on one knee. "Adria?" he voiced. The weary girl took her hands away from her face, and he saw the discomfort in her eyes. Immediately, he stated, "C'mon. Let's put you in bed." He took up her arm and slung it around his shoulders and wrapped his hand around her waist. Helping her get to her feet, Griffin assured, "You're going to be just fine, Adria."

They slowly made their way to the room where Adria resided, and Sable followed behind them. Her steps were short and weak as she leaned on Griffin. "I will be back from the human world in no time," Griffin promised. She tossed her head back and forth in agreement. Laying Adria on her bed, Griffin placed the covers over her as Sable situated the pillow. Griffin stood by her side and grabbed her hand; it was chilled to the bone. "I will be back soon." His blue eyes were filled with anxiety. "Now do you remember what medicine it was that you needed, Adria?"

Adria tried to get the words out but then began to continuously cough once again. With her other hand that was not being held, she placed it over her mouth until it stopped once more. "It's penicillin, Griffin. That is what took it away last time."

Griffin sent her a short, precise nod and stated, "Then penicillin it will be." Griffin let go of her frozen hand, and taking one last look at her, he motioned Sable to follow him outside of the room. They closed the door behind them, standing in the hallway that had the many portraits of the family of the diamond. Griffin crossed his arms. "All right, Sable. When I get through the portal, I am going straight to John's house. He'll be able to help me."

"Of course my, dear boy. I will notify Snolan that you will need her assistance."

"Thank you, Sable," Griffin answered. Sable left the boy to his thoughts. Griffin paced up and down the hallway, growing more apprehensive with every step he took.

A LAST RESORT

As Snolan and Griffin made their departure through the early morning air, Griffin grew very apprehensive. He thought to himself, *What if I don't get back in time?* Quickly he shook these thoughts away, only allowing himself to envision Adria healthy again. "Snolan?" Griffin questioned.

"Yes, Griffin?" Snolan shouted back to him. The dragon was flying at a much swifter rate than usual.

Griffin wrapped his right arm around the neck of the dragon as he let the other arm hang freely. With his left arm, he brushed the front of his hair out of his face that the wind was rustling about. "Did you have any idea that Adria was sick?" The boy paused a bit, thinking and contemplating his next words. "I...I just had no idea, Snolan!"

Snolan swiped her snowy white wings throughout the air with much acceleration. She glanced back at Griffin with her ocean-blue eyes before she worded, "Griffin, Miss Adria did not tell *anyone* of her condition. This is not her fault that she is sick. And this fault surely does not belong to you either, Griffin."

The boy tried to realize all that Snolan was telling him, but even so, Griffin couldn't help but to feel some sort of responsibility for what was happening to her. Once again the boy's mind began wander, *She took care of you, Griffin, and you couldn't even take care of her.* Griffin's mind raced the whole way to the cave and into the human world.

As Griffin and Snolan penetrated the mighty waterfall that rested on the other side of the cave, Griffin brushed some fallen water off his shoulder and sighed, "Back to the human world again."

Snolan shook her head back and forth and rustled her body about shaking the loose water off as well. "We'll only be here shortly, Griffin. Now where is this path to John's house?"

Griffin directed her toward the path that she had dropped him off the last time he made a visit to John's house. However, this time, the surroundings looked much different. The time before this one, Snolan had taken Griffin back to the human world during winter. Now being summer, the air was warm and radiant. The tree branches did not shine with the winter's frost about them but instead glowed and shimmered in the sunlight. Griffin could see the old, overgrown trail in front of them as they flew. He pointed out to Snolan, "There it is!"

The dragon nodded her head, acknowledging the boy. However, she did not slow down; instead, Snolan made a sharp turn on the path in which Griffin had just directed her towards.

"What are you doing, Snolan?" he yelled up to her.

She did not slow down but continued to speed up through the forest, keeping the dirt trail in her sights beneath her. Snolan was an extraordinary flyer. She whizzed in and out of the way of the trees that stood before her pursuit. Her agile movements through the trees got Griffin quickly through the woods much faster than the boy could move on foot. She gained more speed with each minute that passed until the end of the trail revealed itself before them. Finally, the exhausted being soared downward and rested all four feet on the forest's surface. Her mighty chest moved up and down quickly in attempt to regain her lungs. Griffin slid off her back as the dragon got the words out. "Flying you directly here was much faster, my boy."

Griffin patted her on her side as she continued to breathe in the fresh air. He walked over in front of her face and said, "Thank you, Snolan." He looked back to the woods reluctantly, hoping and praying that this forest would be efficient enough to hide the dragon until he returned. Griffin knew that if Snolan were to be seen, it would wreak mayhem and Adria would not see her medicine anytime soon.

John's house could be seen up ahead in a large clearing where the path ended. "Snolan, just wait for me in the woods, okay? I will be no longer than two hours."

Finally regaining her breath, she responded, "I'll be here, Griffin." The boy then left her side and made his way up to John's home.

Once again, the home in which he used to so frequently visit had not changed a bit. And for a split moment, Griffin began to reminisce on the times spent here. The boy thought of the exact day, time, and moment that he realized John was more of a mentor than his actual father would ever be. It was one evening when the sun was just dipping over the horizon before them. At this time Griffin had not spoken to John yet about how he felt about his home life. But Griffin did not have to explain much to him for John to know. They were finishing up their session for the day when John turned to Griffin and stated, "You know, boy, if you ever need time away or somewhere to go, my house is right down the street. You're a great kid. Do not let anyone tell you otherwise."

That was the first time Griffin felt accepted for who he was, something that his immediate family could never give him.

Bringing himself back to reality, Griffin approached the front door to the home where John lived. John had always kept his home neat and cozy with lively roses and marigolds flooding the flowerbeds. However, Griffin did not take anytime appreciating the lovely environment. He pounded his fist across the wooden door that sat before him. Griffin restlessly moved from side to side and fiddled with his hair. "How am I going to explain this one?" He whispered, "A girl that has been missing from this town for more than five years needs medication?" Griffin clasped his open palm across his face in dismay. "Yeah, that sounds great," he said aloud again. The boy then knocked the door a couple more times, growing more anxious with every moment that passed.

Griffin waited impatiently for the next five minutes at the door when he heard a voice from the woods behind him. "Is he not home?"

Griffin swung his body around quickly nearly causing him to topple over. In the forest he could see Snolan's face peering through a thicket. Griffin's eyebrows drew closer together in an irritated scowl and exclaimed in a hushed wording, "Are you crazy!" Griffin flung his hands outward. "Sable will kill me if you are seen!"

The dragon ignored the lecturing boy and continued to speak to him through the bushes. "Well, if he is not here, Griffin, we must request another solution!"

Griffin placed his hands on his hips and gazed at the doorstep where he stood. He knew Snolan was right. Adria needed the medicine straightway, and if John was not home, they could not wait around for him. Griffin slowly made his way off the step and onto the grass. He looked back at the house momentarily then pushed through the forest brush where Snolan resided. Snolan stood on all fours before the boy, her mighty tail lightly swaying from side to side. Griffin let out a sigh, and then clasped his palms together before speaking. "All right, this is the plan." The dragon's eyes lit up as she listened intently. "There is a pharmacy..." Snolan cocked her head to the side in confusion. "It's a place where I can get the medicine." He reworded. "It's just a few miles down the road. You stay here and stay out of sight, Snolan."

As he turned away from her, Snolan released a sizable amount of air through her nostrils. The air was exceedingly warm as it touched the back of Griffin's neck. "Ouch!" He stated, turning to face her and grasping the back of his heated neck.

"Griffin, let me fly you. It will be much faster." Her eyes were hopeful. "Miss Adria does not have time." Dusk was now approaching, and the boy knew each moment that passed was threatening Adria's health.

So once again, they were off. Whizzing throughout the dense forest at full velocity, while Griffin directed her. The boy could barely see the highway through the forest, as he made sure they were flying in route with it. He wrapped his legs tightly around the torso of the dragon's belly and embraced her scaly neck in his arms. Snolan was indeed correct, and they had gotten through the trees much swifter than Griffin could ever move on foot. She touched down on all fours as the pharmacy was now in sight.

Hopping off of her back, the boy began to jog in the direction of the large white building. "I'll be back, Snolan!" he shouted behind him.

The dragon watched Griffin as he made his way out of the forest. He stopped at the edge of the woods and peered around a thick fur tree. A red pickup truck was just leaving the building as Griffin witnessed it driving away. It had been over a year since Griffin had been around modern technology, and he got a funny sensation when seeing trucks and regular stores once again. *Have I really been away for that long?* he asked himself. Refocusing his wandering mind, Griffin thought of how he was going to obtain this medicine. Darkness had well overtaken the evening, and the boy knew the chances of the store being open were very slim, as he didn't observe any activity around it.

Griffin crept around the protecting tree and ran to the parking lot where the front door was. He hopped up the couple stairs that lay before him and gazed through a small window on the white door. The door held many flyers and notices taped around it. Griffin half-expected to see a Missing Persons poster with his face on it. All lights were off, and not a sound was escaping the white walls. It was just as Griffin predicted—the store was not open at this hour. He stood at the doorstep, contemplating his next decision. "Well, better make this quick, Griffin," he spoke to himself.

The boy then retracted his elbow back toward his body and, then in an instant, swung it forward, crashing it through the window.

Brinnnnng, brinnnnng, brinnnnng! The alarm to the pharmacy had sounded immediately. Griffin scrambled to reach through the window that now had broken glass clinging about it. Grasping the door handle on the other side, he rotated the lock, allowing him to open it. Bursting through the door, lights were flashing all around as the alarm continued to blare uncontrollably. Griffin dashed around the front desk to where a switch to an alarm rested. Panicked, he quickly examined the red switch, and in hopes to silence the deafening noise, he pulled the handle downward. As soon as Griffin did this, it did not stop the sounds but instead triggered a whole new alarm system!

"*Noooooooo!*" Griffin shouted, clutching the top of his head, nearly ripping out his shaggy hair. Griffin had now set off the fire alarm as well. He dashed to the back room of the building and found countless cabinets of different kinds of medication. "Penicillin, penicillin," he repeated as he shuffled throughout the different prescription bottles. Griffin tugged the other cabinets ajar as he struggled to find the correct medication. Pill bottles were flying in every direction and smashing to the floor, some breaking open, causing the small tablets to spill about the floor. Suddenly, Griffin could see flashlights from the nearby window. Griffin's already-racing heart sped up even faster as he could now see who was carrying the flashlights. It was the police. Turning back to the numerous pill bottles, he began to shuffle about them once more until he found one that read *Penicillin*.

"Yes!" he yelled gripping the bottle tightly in his palm.

Snolan, who had walked near the edge of the forest to wait for Griffin, was witnessing the whole scene. She hid behind the forest's protecting bushes as she peered her head around them to give herself a good view. The dragon gasped as five cop cars were now parked in the pharmacy's lot, their lights flashing and sirens blazing. The policemen were dressed in all black, with their handguns ready for action. They waited outside the building and shouted, "You have been caught! Come out with your hands up!" Moments later, a fire truck with a long ladder that rested atop it came hurling in the driveway as well.

"What are these creatures?" Snolan expressed under her breath. Never in her days had she seen the technology that the human world contained. And certainly not seeing any vehicles ever before, she could only think that what she was witnessing were large beasts.

Then without warning, Snolan could see Griffin slip out of a side door to the building. But he was seen. The boy dashed toward the woods with the bottle of medicine clinging about in his hands. Griffin glanced behind him to see two officers in his pursuit, their fists clenched and sending threatening words his way. The boy retracted his arm that held the tablets and threw it as far as he could in the direction where Snolan sat waiting for him. The bottle landed a couple feet behind Snolan as she bounded off to acquire it. And just as she picked up the medicine in her mouth, she lifted her head to see three police officers restraining Griffin. "Snolan, *go*!" he shouted. "Leave, Snolan!" Snolan did as she was told and bounded off in the other direction. She took flight and made her way back toward the Critins in an utter panic.

He wrestled with the policemen as they pushed his face in the mud beneath him and confined his hands behind his back. Getting the captured boy to his feet, one policeman stood before him while the other two held him in place. Griffin's face was smudged with dirt as his chest moved violently up and down.

"Well, well, well," the officer smugly began, "looks like we found long-lost Griffin Dominic."

CAPTURED BY HIS OWN KIND

Snolan pierced the massive waterfall with all that her body could conjure. She hurled through the cave as fast as her wings could take her. The cave was dark and damp as usual, as the dragon squinted her eyes and focused on what was ahead. As she made gains back to the Critin castle with the bottle of penicillin tightly locked around her jaws, she only had one thing in mind. *Did I make the right decision?* she hopelessly speculated. Snolan worried that when she returned to the human world to retrieve Griffin, she would have no idea where to find him. Snolan knew of one person that could help her. And that person was John. But how would John take encountering a dragon? *And what if I returned and John was still not home?* she contemplated, as the light at the end of the tunnel was growing larger.

The dragon's wings grew exceptionally fatigued as she nearly collapsed on the cement flooring in front of the two castle doors. Snolan's heart battered up and down in her chest as she lay on the ground. She dropped the bottle of medication to the floor, allowing her to take in deeper breaths. Bringing her mighty body back on her feet, she slowly walked to the castle doors and positioned her head downward. She then allowed the tip of her white horns to knock against the wooden door. Moments later, the door was being opened as Sable stood before Snolan.

"Just in the nick of time, my dear! Adria has worsened." Opening the other door so Snolan could step through, he questioned. "Where is the medicine?" Still regaining her breaths, Snolan nodded her head to the bottle that was lying on ground. The container had clear slime about it from being carried in Snolan's mouth. "Why is there saliva all about this?" Sable had a disgusted look about his face as he flung his talon to the side of him releasing the slobber.

"Sable," Snolan began, "I had to bring the medicine back. They took Griffin!"

Immediately the revolted impression the diamond bearer had turned into a worried and baffled illustration. He took a quick step toward Snolan and expressed, "What do you mean? Who took him, Snolan?"

Snolan thrashed her head from side to side as Sable followed her with his eyes. "It was bad, it was so bad." She wept. "Griffin had to get into this white building. And when he did, sounds started invading the air! Then these huge creatures with lights all around them appeared in the pathway, bringing different sounds of their own!" She paused for a moment. Sable's mouth was gaping open, revealing his forked tongue. "Then other humans dressed in all black jumped out of the large light-filled monsters and took Griffin! He had just enough time to throw me the bottle..."

Sable then began to pace back and forth before the flustered creature. Sable then gripped onto his head, with his talons causing tiny feathers to float to the ground. "Why would his *own* kind treat him like this? This is preposterous!" Sable roared, with his emotions rising.

"I don't know!" Snolan added. "I did not think Griffin was doing anything sinful! He merely went in the white structure and then departed and then all this fuss was underway! But I am going back for him, Sable. If I can just speak with John, I am certain he will have knowledge of where to find Griffin. It's our only solution!"

And there Griffin was, captured and caged behind a barred large wall, like an untamed animal of the woods. He sat on a cool cement block, with his head slouched over, hands on his forehead with his fingers intertwined about his dirt-smudged hair. His brown handcrafted trousers were tattered and a bit torn from the struggle with the policemen, and his green shirt was anything but clean. Even though the boy was imprisoned, with no plan of action, he could only think of one thing. And that one thing was whether or not Adria received the medicine she so desperately needed. "Snolan *had* to have heard me," he whispered. The jail he was in contained no one else. This was where they temporarily kept the convicts until they decided what to do with them or which county jail to place them in. Also, outside Griffin's jail was a black desk with stacks of paper and picture frames atop it.

In an instant, Griffin jerked his head upward to the sound of a door being propped open. This was not the door to Griffin's cell, but instead the door that rested outside his prison. First, through the entrance came the very officer who had recognized him earlier. He had a devilish grin hanging about his cheeks, the kind of smile someone would give off in a time of vengeance. Next through the door was someone Griffin would shudder at the sight of. This was the very person he hoped he would *never* lay eyes on again. This person was the one who drove him out of the human world and made his childhood a despicable nightmare.

Through the opening, following the officer was Griffin's father, David Dominic. The boy's eyes expanded to full capacity, and his heart dropped to the floor. His palms immediately began to perspire as anxiety set it, blocking off all other emotions. David looked the same as he always did—his broad shoulders larger than ever, his black eyes no more inviting than a hungry black bear. The rugged man walked over to Griffin's jail cell slowly, keeping his shadowy eyeballs on Griffin's horrified face. He stopped before the bars and crossed his arms. "Thought I'd never have to look at you again, boy." His voice was forceful. "And here you are."

Griffin did not say a word. He was immobile where he sat, incapable to bring about a single movement, and unable to get out a single word. David began to pace back and forth in front of Griffin. The policeman stood a few yards behind the scene, still owning the menacing smile. Then David stopped in his tracks and moved his face closer to the bars of the cell. He was examining Griffin's face. David turned his head to one side and, with his fingertips, motioned the officer to come closer. "Do you have contacts in?" David questioned. Griffin said nothing and stared blankly ahead. "Answer me, boy!"

The officer then wrenched the set of keys from his waistband and shuffled them about until he found the one that would unlock Griffin's door. Shoving the correct key through the keyhole, he unlocked the door and grabbed Griffin by the arm, yanking him out of the prison. Once again, the officer restrained Griffin and held him directly in front of his father. The policemen mouthed a sickening verse, "I believe your father asked you a question, you coward!"

Griffin's chest moved up and down in a violent pattern. Adrenaline shot through his veins, striking his senses. He lifted his head, so he was now nearly eye level with his father, and stated, "No, I do *not* have contacts in." His whitish-blue eyes looked straight through David's dark ones.

David moved his head back in utter shock as the policeman positioned himself in front of Griffin so he could examine the boy himself. "David, he's not wearing contacts."

David clenched his fist and exclaimed, "Well! He must he on some kind of drugs then! Just look at the wretched scar across his face! Who knows what he's been doing this past year!"

The policemen then pricked a few hairs off of Griffin's head. "Let's see what kind of drugs he's been on." Then with one hand wrapped around the boy's neck he walked Griffin back to the cell. Pushing the boy in, he then securely locked the door, leaving Griffin imprisoned once more. The two of them started their way out of the room. And just before David's full body was out, he peered his face back in and stated, "Your mother did not even want to come down and see you, Griffin. I just came to see that you were behind bars—where you belong." Griffin made no eye contact as the man slammed the door behind him, leaving Griffin alone once again.

AN UNEXPECTED ENCOUNTER

John had just returned from a weeklong camping trip with his wife, Cindy. They were finishing up unpacking their truck that held all of their supplies, tent, fishing gear, and, of course, enough arrows and targets for John to keep busy on the trip. John took a bow and plenty of arrows wherever he went. This was his passion that he had passed along to Griffin many years ago. However, John had not the slightest knowledge that this craving for archery he taught Griffin was now the choice weaponry for a species he did not know existed. John knew that Griffin had been up to something extraordinary, something that was unexplainable, but he did not know what.

Cindy had just left for town to get some steaks for dinner. So while Cindy was away at the market, John hacked some wood by the forest nearby that they could use to cook their meal. He set up the round logs upon an old tree stump and thrust the axe into it, slicing it precisely into two pieces. He did this many times until the man had a generous woodpile next to him.

He lifted the sharp axe over his right shoulder, and just before driving it into the piece of wood before him, he heard, "John…" The voice was hesitant and quiet. He held the axe in the air as he looked from side to side. And then he heard nothing. Shrugging his shoulders, he got ready to make contact with the log once more. And just as he released the axe from the position he had it in, he heard the voice again, "John!" This time it was louder, alarming John; it caused him to completely miss the piece, driving the metal into the stump the wood rested on.

The man let go of the axe handle and stepped backward from the woods in a hurry. His fist was held in front of his face, his body crouched over like a preying tiger. "Who...whose there!" he demanded. The man's brown eyes shifted from side to side as he attempted to witness who was throwing words his way.

"Please do not be frightened," the voice spoke. And now John knew it was coming from the direction of his backyard woods.

Fists still raised and ready for action, John shouted into the forest, "You best then reveal yourself!" John looked at his fists and then to the axe that was sticking out from the tree stump. Feeling irrational, he hurriedly ran to his axe and took it up in his hand. "I have a weapon in hand that I will use if it be necessary!"

"Please, John, I am a friend of Griffin's." The voice was gentle and nurturing.

John took in large breaths as he tried to contain himself. As he continued to shift his eyes in every direction, he shouted back to the mysterious voice, "Well...if ye be a friend of Griffin's, then...then where be the boy! Expose yourself!" John gripped the axe tighter as his hands grew sweaty.

"That is precisely why I have come to you, John." And before another moment could pass, the bushes that sat before the terrified man began to rustle about. John took a step backward, and as he did, coming through the forest that lay in front of him was a massive prehistoric being. It was Snolan. The dragon's beaming scales glistened like gems of the sea, and her soft blue eyes reflected John's image in them.

John said nothing but, instead, stood before Snolan, eyes widened to full length and jaw descending to the floor. And as a few more moments passed, John found his legs and started to stumble backwards. Then with no prior notice, John let out an ear-piercing wail, "*Ahhhhhhhhh!*" Immediately, the man dropped his axe in front of the dragon and turned to sprint up the steps to his house.

"Wait!" Snolan cried. "John, I am not going to harm you!" The man made it to his front doorstep, bursting through the door, causing one of the hinges to break loose. John slammed the half-broken door behind him, waiting on the other side of the entrance for any sign of the beast.

"What is this? What is going on?" John whispered to himself as his heart was a constant flutter. "Griffin has some explaining to do!"

"That all can be done if we find him!" Snolan was peering her head through one of the opened windows to John's home.

"*Ahhhhhhh!*" John shouted once more then shuffled over to the kitchen dinette, taking up a wooden chair in his hands for protection. "Why are ye here!" the man demanded.

Snolan's lengthy neck was protruding over the kitchen sink. There was a pool of water beneath her, causing her vibrant scales to reflect in frenzy. "I am here because they took Griffin. Our land needs him back, John!"

Chair still raised above his head, like a chimpanzee claiming its territory, John replied, "Who took Griffin? What land?"

Snolan took a step forward from the outside, allowing her head to move closer to John. "Please let me explain."

John knew that if a being of her stature wanted to harm him, she could have easily done so by now. Besides, this was not John's first time seeing Snolan for he caught a meager glimpse of Griffin and her flying away the last time Griffin visited him. He had questioned himself if he had truly witnessed such a thing—now he knew what he saw was accurate. "Okay." John placed the chair down, and Snolan's mouth transformed into a grin, showing off her enlarged teeth. "I will meet ye outside to hear what ye have to say. But my wife will be returning soon. This must be quick."

Snolan nodded her head in agreement and raced to meet John outside. They met down by the forest's edge. Snolan explained to John what had happened at the pharmacy. She told him of Adria and how sick she was and how badly she needed the medicine. "The medicine is back with Adria, and she is mending well, John. But we need Griffin back." She paused a moment. "Can you just give Griffin one thing? One thing and...and I will be able to find him."

John scratched his rough chin with the tips of his fingers and expressed, "What is it that he needs?"

"It's hanging about my neck." Snolan had the whistle used to call her dangling down by her chest on a golden chain. The whistle was sleek and thin, and shimmered with a green tint to it. Snolan lowered her head down so John could slide it off of her.

John took the piece up in his hand, examining it. "Will Griffin know what to do?"

"Yes"—she smiled—"tell him a friend wanted him to have it. He'll know what to do."

John continued to scrutinize the object he had just obtained from a dragon. Looking back to her, he lightly swayed his head back and forth and chuckled to himself in disbelief.

"I know you have many unanswered questions, John."

"You think!" the man responded.

"Griffin will be able to explain himself, John. But I need to get him back first." The dragon then began to shift her body toward the forest. "Please see to it that the boy receives that whistle. I'll be waiting."

John watched her as she disappeared into the thick woods.

A moment later, John's wife, Cindy, pulled into the driveway and saw him standing by the woodpile at the threshold of the forest. John quickly shoved the whistle into his jean pocket and took the fallen axe up in his hand. Cindy stepped out of the red SUV and stated, "You're still cutting wood?"

John nervously stuttered, "Yeah, sorry, honey! I got a bit sidetracked!"

THE RESULTS

Griffin had been captured in temporary lockup for over a day. He began to wonder if he would ever go back to Aranwea, see the Critins or Adria. Griffin did have some sense of hope though. And that hope was the mere fact that he was not stuck with the Shriekian this time, captured and tortured for their amusement. Even though he was physically no longer tortured, his heart was filled with anxiety in wondering if the medicine had made it to Adria in time. This made Griffin uneasy, unable to relax or get a moment's rest.

The boy shoved his hands deep into his pant pockets and strolled about the room, looking for anything that could bring him an escape plan. All the prison contained was an old, rusty sink that had water dribbling from the spout, an old, musty bed that was discolored in every corner of it, and an ancient-looking toilet. As Griffin walked about the tiny barred cage, the door to the outside of the room began to open. The boy took his hands from his pockets and hurriedly sat down on the uninviting bed. Through the door was the officer, and in the officer's hand rested a folder that on the top of it read, *Results*. Following the policeman was no one other than Griffin's father. The boy rolled his eyes at the sight of him. "You can ask Griffin yourself!" The officer raged.

"Fine, I will!" David spouted. He then made his way to the jail cell where Griffin dwelled. "Look at me, boy." David was chewing a piece of gum, grinding it between his jaws loud enough to be heard for miles. His black eyes showed no mercy as he stood firmly before him, with his arms crossed and chest puffed. "What drugs have you been taking, boy?"

For the first time, Griffin turned his head to acknowledge his father. He spoke with force, "Why should I answer to you?"

Surprised by the boy's reaction, David became remarkably enraged and gripped the bar in front of him, "How dare you speak to me in such ways!" David spit the gum he was chewing through the jail, just missing the boy's pant leg.

Griffin abruptly hoisted himself from the bed and stood in alignment to David. The only thing keeping them from each other was the metal bars. "You have *no* right claiming me as your son. You have made my life a nightmare since day one! You are not worth the words that are coming from my mouth!" Griffin's tension was rising. He could feel the tiny hairs on his arms standing on edge as his white-blue eyes penetrated David's black soul. "Nor are you worthy of standing before me in my presence! You want to know why I left? Huh? Do ya?" Griffin could hear his own heart beating throughout his chest and consuming his eardrums. "I left because I found somewhere better, *much better*. And I sure as heck did not leave because I wanted to do drugs!" Then Griffin moved away from where David stood, turning his back to his father.

David, for the first time, was speechless. He could only stand there, his fists clenched around the bars with his son's back to him. Trying to speak, the man started, "Yeah! Well—"

"What do the results state?" Griffin interrupted the man.

"I don't believe that is your business, boy," David replied as he released his hands from the jail cell.

"Hmmmmm"—Griffin sarcastically placed his finger beneath his chin as if contemplating a great subject—"since when does my own health not become my business?" Griffin moved to the side so the policeman was better in his view. "Please enlighten us, officer. What do the results to my drug test say?"

The officer began to shuffle throughout the papers and muttered a few words under his breath. Finding the words, he said exasperatedly, "It states that you are clean."

Griffin shifted his head upward and sang, "Whooooooo!" The boy then began to slowly clap his hands together, making his way toward the front of the jail cell.

His father looked utterly disgusted at Griffin. "Yeah well whatever the results say, I know otherwise! I know what you have been into, boy!"

"You have *no* idea what I have been into." Griffin smirked, showing off his white teeth. "But it surely has not been drugs."

David took one last grimacing look at his son. The man then turned and stormed out of the building, leaving the policeman and Griffin to themselves. Griffin felt an overwhelming sensation that he had never felt before. He had finally stood up to his father and told him how miserable he felt toward him. This was something Griffin had wanted to do for years now but never had the chance to.

"Well, Griffin Dominic"—the officer looked through the papers once again—"I do not know how you suddenly changed your eye color, and to be honest, I do not care." The man paused for a moment; Griffin was still in his trance of self-satisfaction. "But that does not redeem you from breaking and entering. Since you are not eighteen years of age for another month, you will be sentenced to McClairen Penitentiary for Boys." The man scratched the back of his head and looked toward the door. "You will leave tomorrow morning to go to McClairen. Until then, you have one last visitor."

The last words the man spoke of caught Griffin's attention as he lightly tossed his head from each side, regaining his awareness. "Another visitor?" Griffin gasped. "Who is it?" And before he could get another word out, the officer stepped to the side, and through the doors came a familiar face. It was John. Griffin heart rose with gladness at the sight of him. He grabbed the top of his head and stated, "No way, John!" Griffin motioned the man to come over by his side.

"You have two minutes!" the policeman stated and then left the room shutting the door behind him.

John smiled at Griffin as he made his way to the cell. The large man was wearing his normal baggy pair of jeans and red flannel shirt. His face was half shaved and untidy, and his boots brought in some dirt particles. John planted himself before Griffin, crossing his arms and giving Griffin a rather disapproving look. Griffin grew worried and spouted off, "I...I can explain, John..." John put his hand in front of Griffin motioning him to stop talking. Then John rustled his hand in his right front pocket and pulled out the whistle. "Wha...what? How did you get—"

Finally John spoke to the boy. "Your friend told me to give you this, young man. She said you would know what to do."

Griffin was mesmerized as he nearly forgot to breathe the air before him. "My...my friend?"

"Yes, Griffin. Ye have some strange...and rather large friends." John chuckled a bit and stuck his hand through the barred cell with the whistle hanging about it. Griffin opened the palm of his hand and allowed John to drop the chain. "You do know what to do, do you not, Griffin?"

Griffin nodded his head up and down. He placed Snolan's whistle in his pocket then turned to John once more, "How did you come across this, John?"

"I was sought out, Griffin. I am just the one delivering the message."

"Thank you, John. I have so much to explain to you. If I only had—"

John once again placed his hand in the air as if he were directing traffic. "In time I will know, Griffin," John spoke quietly. "But this be not the time." John leaned in closer toward the bars where Griffin stood behind. "I only have one request."

Griffin propped himself closer as well, shifting his head so John could be heard more efficiently. "Of course, John. Anything."

"Before you leave back to where you have been, make a pit stop at the old house, would ya?" John backed away from Griffin as the boy nodded his head up in down in agreement.

"Two minutes are up!" the officer sneered, standing in the doorway; brows squinted with a face of impatience. John began to walk away from Griffin, making his way to where the officer stood. "You'll be spending the night here, boy." John waited to hear all the man was speaking of before completely exiting the area. "So tomorrow morning, you will be transported straight to McClairen Penitentiary for Boys."

John took one last look at the caged boy and then left. The policeman closed the door behind him.

DRAGONS

Griffin tossed and turned in the night. The bed in which he rested emitted a horrendous fragrance and was also as pleasant as sleeping upon sharpened stakes. Griffin found himself in a half asleep, and half awake dream. Everything was foggy. Shadows passed left and right as only their silhouettes could be seen. Sweat permeated out of his pores as the dream became more vivid. His body lobbed from left to right on the uncomfortable mattress with much force. He gripped onto his shaggy hair, and with one last violent pull of his body, he was off the bed and on the cement floor of the cell.

He opened his eyes, but when he did, he did not see the ominous jail cell in which he so certainly knew he lingered in, but instead, he saw thick and unleveled stone beneath him. "What?" he gasped. He looked as though he was atop some kind of mountainous landscape. All was bright and nearly blinding him; although it was vivid, the boy could see clouds and haze blocking his eyesight. Still lying on the floor, Griffin rubbed his eyes continuously in hopes to awaken from this mysterious fantasy.

Griffin unsealed his eyelids yet again, and when he did, he did not see the dense fog that he had witnessed prior. Instead, he saw billowing flames before him, gathering more strength and stature with every moment that passed. Griffin was not afraid of these flares though, and instead of fear creeping into his essence, he felt comfort seeping into his soul. Griffin reached his hand out toward the fire, and when he did, all flames had deceased, leaving a heap of smoke to pass. The boy, still lying on the cool mountain-like terrain, squinted his eyes for he could see shadowy figures now coming into view. Griffin pushed his hands beneath his chest and found his legs, still keeping his eyes on the many silhouettes before him.

All smoke had disappeared, and stepping forward was one of the many figures. The large beast stepped toward him with one tremendous claw at a time. Coming into better view now, Griffin stood before a mighty red dragon. Her wings were a lighter tint of red as the rest of her body was consumed in rose-colored red. The eyes of the being were soft and a deep yellow. Her horns jetted back beautifully, followed by black spikes leading down to the tip of her immense tail. The dragon demanded, "Where is the leader of our kind?"

"I...I don't..." Griffin stuttered greatly and moved backward. And as he did, he looked behind him to see a giant cliff. Trying to regain his balance, the boy flailed his arms up and down, but even though he did, he found himself toppling over the side of the mountain. "*Noooooo!*" he shouted. Just before hitting the ground, Griffin awakened, finding himself drenched in sweat and lying on the floor to the jail cell he had been confined in. He placed his right hand over his chest, gripping his t-shirt. The boy took in profound, unending breaths as he attempted to calm his shaking body down. "What was...?" he worded aloud. "What was that a dream...or was that a vision?" Usually the boy's visions were brought on in broad daylight, with no chance of him mistaking it for a dream, but this time he was uncertain what had just occurred exactly. His body felt uneasy and shaky like they usually did when he had visions, but still he could not be sure.

Griffin replayed the dream and/or visions back in his head time and time again. The red dragon's image was engrained in his mind, like a broken record replaying the same track. "Where is the leader of our kind?" Griffin recalled the dragon's words. "What does this mean?" he contemplated. It was merely three o'clock in the morning as Griffin rolled back onto the creaky bed and made an attempt to find sleep; however, this was not possible for the boy. All Griffin could do was ponder this mysterious dream or vision. He wanted and needed to know what it meant and how this could change what was yet to come.

Two hours later, it was very early morning. Griffin had not moved an inch since the odd encounter earlier. Then without prior notice, two officers came through the door. Griffin sat up immediately, seeing the two men coming. The two cops were wearing their normal attire—dark pants with a matching top, black glossy boots, and a badge polished so efficiently that it could blind a passerby. Griffin impatiently waited for them, in hopes that they had come to transfer him. The policeman had said they would be transporting him early in the morning, but Griffin did not expect them at this hour for it was only five o'clock a.m.

Griffin asked them, "Are you here to take me to the boy's institution?" The men did not reply, instead they made their way to the cell where Griffin resided and began to shuffle through a ring full of keys. "Guess so," he whispered under his breath.

"Why else would we be here, huh?" one of the officers dryly specified. This man was shorter and rounder than a healthy pumpkin during Halloween season. The other was tall and skinny with black hair that jetted from front to back like he was in some kind of John Travolta film. Neither of them Griffin had seen before. "C'mon, boy." Each of them took up one of Griffin's arms and escorted him to their cop car that had the backseat door already ajar.

The car was nothing special; it was rusted in some areas with gray tires and had scratched paint across it. Griffin felt nearly insulted that he would be taken away in such a vehicle. But then again, he reminded himself, *I guess we are in Oakridge.* Griffin sat down in the black cushioned seat as one of them closed the door. Making their way forward, they opened the front two doors and got in.

Griffin could hear them muttering stuff under their breaths. One of them worded in a hush tone, "They were right...he *does* have freaky blue eyes."

The other officer nodded his head up and down like a bobblehead on a busy dashboard. "Yeah, and they say he was clean!"

Griffin sat back and smiled to himself, boasting a bit at the conversation he was overhearing. He felt as though he were some kind of mysterious bandit that was on the run and finally captured. Griffin always had a rebellious side to him, and these thoughts pleased him. What Griffin did not know was that he was much more than this. Griffin's return had the people of Oakridge buzzing! Radio stations and news channels picked up the scoop on a boy who had gone missing over a year ago and returned with impossible blue eyes. He had the whole town in an uproar, and Griffin had only been back for a little over two days!

The morning was still young, and the sun had barely begun to peer its face out over the horizon. It was twilight. Griffin gazed about his surroundings. They looked to be driving in the middle of nowhere. No one else was on the road as they drove down a long, straight two-lane highway. To the left was a large field of vegetable plants that consumed the landscape. On the right was nothing but a large uninhabited field.

The two officers in the front seat were squabbling over some nonsense about what had just happened in an episode of a TV series they both watched. The plumper one was certain that his partner was wrong and that he was willing to place money on the line to prove it. Then unexpectedly, they both stopped talking due to a high-pitched sound coming from the backseat. The heavier officer in the passenger seat swung his head around where Griffin was. The other continued to glance back, keeping his eyes on the road. He saw Griffin with the whistle in his mouth.

"What do you think you are doing?" the short one exclaimed.

Griffin did not respond and did not seem the least bit affected by this question. He just kept pressing his lips to the piece, taking in a chest full of air, and again sending that air through the whistle as hard and fast as his lungs would allow him.

"Hey!" the one who was driving shouted back to him. "Did ya hear the man? Stop that noise!"

"This is not the time to make music!" The pudgy officer was now mocking Griffin. "No matter what, you're still going to that institute. No stupid whistle will save you, foolish boy!"

Griffin stopped sending air through the device. He placed the whistle back in his pocket as the cop kept laughing in his face, turning into an annoying cackle.

"You're right," Griffin declared.

The cop ceased his aggravating outburst.

"The whistle will not save me"—Griffin looked straight into the man's eyes—"but Snolan will."

Before either of the policemen could say another word, the roof of their car caved in like a meager shell being cracked. The windshield crumbled before their faces as the cop car spun out of control, burning rubber all about the cement and causing smoke to fill the air.

"*What is going on!*" the cop screamed, trying to keep his car under control as they spun in circles, an out-of-control merry-go-round. Griffin, who did not have a safety belt on, was being thrashed from side to side about the backseat of the car until they finally came to a stop. The men up front were cowering and whimpering with their arms folded over their heads as if the sky itself were collapsing. The ceiling of the car was nearly touching the headrests as it was badly damaged. "What is going on!" the same cop spoke. "S...s...something must have fallen on us!"

Griffin, who was now on the floor of the car half upside down, used his arms to hoist him up right. Brushing some fallen debris off his shoulders and hair, he could see the two men still cowering. And when he gazed out of the broken window to his right, he saw a familiar shadow fly overhead. "Snolan!" Griffin called.

With some work, Griffin was able to open the broken car door. He stumbled out of the vehicle, waving his arms up and down like a lost traveler on a deserted island. And just as Griffin predicted, it was Snolan. It was not easy for him to see her in the early morning light, but Griffin knew it was her and could spot Snolan under any condition. With a quick tug of her white wings, she nose-dived to the ground, landing but twenty yards from the vehicle in which Griffin stood.

Griffin ran to her; grabbing her neck, he swung his leg around her torso. "Yes, Snolan!" Griffin hysterically cried. "You did it! Let's go!" Griffin patted her rough neck; however, she did not move a single muscle. Instead, Snolan's head slowly sunk as she stared directly at the cop car, her tail lightly swaying back and forth with concentration. Griffin questioned, "Snolan, what are you doing?" The boy was growing concerned. "Quick before they see you!"

As soon as these words had left his lips, the two cops came stumbling out of the car, their arms held high, positioning a handgun straight at Griffin and Snolan. Their jaws dropped to the floor at the sight of Snolan. Getting a better view, the thinner one moved a bit closer and removed his glasses from his face. Utter shock shot through the veins of the two men. Snolan took one step toward them, and before they could respond, she enlarged her cheeks to their full capacity. The two men looked at each other then dropped their hands to the side and started sprinting in opposite directions, wailing and carrying on as if they had just witnessed the impossible—which to them was the impossible.

Snolan let loose the inferno she had built up in her lungs. It was a complete and absolute wall of flames hurling toward the cop car that Griffin had just ridden in moments ago. The blazing fire first hit the front of the car where the engine resided, causing it to ignite immediately bursting into flames. It was the grand finale on the Fourth of July. Snolan took a few steps backward as the heat from the explosion was lightly stroking their faces.

"Satisfied?" Griffin yelled to her.

Snolan grinned as she started to pump her wings. "Very."

They made their way to the forest where they could not be seen, and left the pile of steel to burn on the endless highway.

AN EXPLANATION

Snolan weaved through the woods with ease. It was a never-ending maze that engulfed them as they dodged the overhanging branches of the trees. As Griffin directed her left and right, he shouted up to her so the dragon could hear efficiently, "Did the medicine make it to Adria?" He awaited Snolan's next words with apprehensive building up inside of him.

Snolan lightly tilted her head back and replied, "Yes, Griffin!"

Griffin who was practically leaning off of the dragon to intercept her words, closed his eyes and let out a sigh of relief. He sat back up and secured himself for the flight once more. "Thank you, Snolan."

Thirty minutes later, John's petite home could be seen up ahead through the dense woods. Snolan plummeted to the ground in a small clearing that she could reside in while Griffin visited John. He jumped off her scaly back and pushed through some nearby thickets. The boy's heart began to flutter as he walked through the grass, approaching the front door. Griffin ran his fingers through his black hair, gripping the back of it in dismay. "What am I going to tell him...?" Griffin questioned aloud. "What does he need to know? What *can* he know?" These were all inquiries to which he had no remedy. Griffin advanced closer to the cement steps that rested before John's front door. He stopped and got ready to bang his fist on the door. Shutting his eyes, Griffin inhaled a deep breath. And just before knocking, the front door opened. Griffin, caught off guard, quickly opened his eyes and took a step backward to see John standing on the other side of the doorway. "Hey...hey, John."

The man looked to Griffin and then reluctantly smiled, "Well, that whistle *did* do the trick, now didn't it?" John stepped out of the building, closing the door behind him and Griffin. "I saw you come outta' the woods. Your escape is all over the news, Griff!"

"What?" Griffin cried, gripping the back of his head even harder, nearly pulling out his hair.

"Yeah!" John replied. "The only thing you got going for you is that the two policemen that were transporting you claimed their car was attacked by a 'flying airborne beast,' and no one's buying that story just yet." John chuckled to himself. However, Griffin did not. Instead, he displayed a horrified look upon his face. John saw the dismay in the boy's face and continued, "It would be in your best luck to get out of here, Griff. I assume they're already out lookin' for ya."

Griffin ignored the man and spouted off in a panic, "John, Snolan has been seen! Do you know what this means? I have put a threat on the whole land of Aranwea...!"

John grasped Griffin's right shoulder, turning the distraught boy to him. "Aran-what? What land?"

Griffin shook his head from left to right. "We have much to discuss, John. But it cannot be discussed here." Griffin pondered to himself for a moment until he was struck with an idea. "Want to see a waterfall?"

John turned his head to one side and asked, "And what would be our means of transportation?"

Griffin grinned at the man and stated, "C'mon." He hopped off the steps and began to walk toward the clearing where he left Snolan. John followed behind him. They pushed through the forest brush for a few yards and then found Snolan waiting patiently.

"Well, we meet again, John," the dragon greeted.

"Indeed we do, Snolan." The man gazed at her in amazement.

"Did you guys already discuss all that needed to be said, Griffin?" she questioned.

"Well," Griffin started, "not *exactly*." Snolan intercepted his intentions and scowled at him in disapproval. "Just a flight to the waterfall, Snolan! Maybe if you hadn't made a mile-high smoke signal along the freeway, we wouldn't have to get out of here so quickly!"

Snolan rolled her ocean-blue eyes at the boy and responded, "All right, to the waterfall, then we will be on our way back to Aranwea."

John and Griffin flew on the back of Snolan through the forest. "Are...are you sure about this, Griffin?" John nervously yelled with his legs tightly wrapped around the belly of the dragon.

Griffin laughed to himself at John's panic. The boy started, "We are just taking you to the entrance of the portal, and then Snolan will quickly fly you back."

"Portal?" he questioned with his eyes gazing beneath him at the passing forest floor.

The boy breathed, "We have a lot to talk about." Griffin began to explain his disappearance for the last year. And this time, he did not hold back. He told John of the mysterious red light in the forest that he had been drawn to. Griffin described to the man the whole land of Aranwea, the vile Shriekian, and the family of the Critins. During their conversation, John did not say much. He simply nodded his head at certain remarks Griffin stated and listened intently to the best of his abilities.

"And...and there's this diamond." Griffin eagerly spoke. "And I was brought to Aranwea to help protect it. Well...turns out I was meant to do a lot more than protect a diamond!"

"Wait, wait, wait," John interrupted as he flailed his arms to the sides for a moment but then swiftly placed his arms beneath him on the airborne dragon, regaining his balance. "What are you 'protecting' them with, Griffin?"

Griffin's face lit up like the northern lights themselves. This was the solitary moment that Griffin had been longing for. He had replayed telling John that the Critins' now choice weaponry was a bow and arrow time and time again, but the moment had not come until now. "Well, John, what is the *only* type of weapon that I know how to use?" Griffin chuckled.

John pondered to himself for a moment but then realized in an instant. "You taught them how to use bows and arrows!" John was ecstatic. He threw his arms up, causing him to get off balance once more.

Griffin explained to him about the Critin army and how he had been teaching them the ways of the bow for some time now. John was in utter astonishment. "*You* have been teaching an army?" Griffin nodded his head as he continued to mesmerize John. It was hard for this man to truly grasp all that Griffin was making known to him. It wasn't that he did not believe the boy; even though he trusted Griffin with all his might, it was still hard for John to wrap his mind around such things. The boy then began to explain the reason for returning to the human world this time. He let John know it was not by choice this time and that he no longer felt the temptation of the Shriekian lingering about him.

"And that is why I came back," Griffin expressed. "Adria was sick, and if I did not get medicine to her soon, she could have died. And that is why I broke into the pharmacy." The waterfall could be seen up ahead through the thick trees in which they flew. Hundreds of gallons of water billowed over the falls as Snolan lowered them with every brush of her wings. "See! That is the portal!" They were atop the waterfall, and Griffin was remembering his first ride here with Golydon.

John used his hand as a visor to allow himself to get a better view. He voiced, "That's Salt Creek Falls! I've been here many times!" John's mouth widened into a smile as he spoke to Griffin, "Did you not know that?"

Griffin was astounded. "What? You've been here before, John?" Snolan sailed over the large body of water, causing mist to pat their faces.

"Sure have! I used to go here all the time as a lad. Hiked the whole way through the woods," John replied.

Snolan landed to the side of the basin to the mighty falls. Griffin spouted, "And here I thought I was going to show you something completely different!" Griffin first slid off her back and landed on some uneven rocks, which nearly caused him to topple into the water. John cautiously swung his leg off to the side of the dragon and jumped onto the small rock bed.

"It's okay. Revealing to me where you have been this past year has been different enough for one day," John joked and ruffled Griffin's head with his hand. "I know you best be going, Griff."

Griffin nodded his head and replied, "Snolan can take you back. I'll just wait for her."

John moved his head from side to side. "I know how to get home from here."

Snolan looked to John and reassured, "John, it's really all right. I would not mind giving you a ride home."

John looked to the ground at the passing water beneath him. His reflection showed vividly in the late morning's sun. "I think one flight with a dragon is enough for an old man like me." The man grinned as he placed his hand softly on Snolan's side. "Besides, I think a long... long walk is in order." John then turned to Griffin, who was looking off into the distance. He did not want to leave John after all that he had exposed to him. He wished to converse more with him, answering all of John's questions that he surely had. "Griffin?" The boy slowly moved his face around to see John. "You have found something that truly defies all that humankind has ever known." He paused for a moment as Griffin nodded his head. "Take care of yourself, and if you ever need anything, anything at all, you know where to find me."

Griffin started, "You are about all I have left in the human world, John. I will see you again, and thank you again for all that you have done for me. Without you, I could not have taught the Critins how to use a bow and arrow. Their victory rests within you too."

John graciously smiled at Griffin and then patted him on his shoulder. "You best be going before the whole police force makes its way to ya." John stepped away from Griffin and directed his words to Snolan. "Keep this young man outta' trouble, my dear!"

Snolan looked to Griffin and back to John and replied, "Will do, sir!"

The man took one last glance toward Griffin and the dragon and then turned and made his way from the river. The two of them watched John as he hiked into the woods out of their sight.

"You ready, Griffin?" Snolan cautiously asked.

Griffin was still gazing off into the direction that John had just left him. "Yeah..." the boy responded at last. "Let's go."

DREAM VISIONS

Snolan and Griffin arrived back at the Critin castle in the mid afternoon. The sun's rays were at the highest point of the day as they landed before the two castle doors. Griffin pushed through the doors, entering the structure. He walked past the kitchen in the castle to find Sable, Mogol, and the two army leaders, Schmight and Carlzar, around the egg-shaped table. "And the boy has returned!" Mogol rejoiced, throwing his talons in the air. All sat up immediately and greeted Griffin.

"Snolan allowed us to know what had occurred, Griffin," Sable began. "You were taken by beasts with blinking lights!"

Griffin snickered a bit under his breath and replied, "Yes, Sable, that is what happened." The boy joined them at the table and told them what had occurred. He explained to them why he was delayed and the reason behind him being captured by his own kind.

Sable was positioned at the head of the table, his talons clasped together resting upon the surface. The diamond bearer leaned in closer and, protruding his beak toward the middle, retorted, "Snolan was not seen now...was she?"

Griffin stuttered, "Ummmm..." He shifted his eyes from left to right. All at the table were staring him down, like he was some kind of animal in an exhibit. "Sable...when she broke me free of those flashing lit beasts...two other humans did happen to see her..." Griffin squinted his eyes as he winced and awaited Sable's response.

"This will not do, my boy!" Sable roared. "This will not do at all! She has been seen?" Sable pushed his chair back and stood up abruptly.

Griffin took a stand as well and boldly replied, "There was *no* other way, Sable!" Griffin's eyebrows drew in and his teeth clenched after he spoke. The other three beings at the table looked at each other as their uneasiness exceeded greatly.

"Well, Griffin, if that be the case, so be it. But this whole land has now been at risk, and we must seek out a solution." Sable stopped his words as Griffin stood in place. The diamond bearer then dismissed himself from the table and stormed out the castle doors.

Griffin slumped his head down and released air through his nostrils. "There was no other way."

Mogol, who was sitting across from Griffin at the edge of his seat through the whole discussion reassured, "I know it was not intentional, my boy."

Griffin then moved the dining room chair off to the side and questioned, "Where is Adria?"

"She's in her room. She's nearly fully recovered," Mogol ended. Griffin pushed the chair in and left their company.

Griffin trampled through the hallway with much irritation on his mind. *What was I supposed to do!* he contemplated. Griffin knew why

Sable was concerned, but he did not *intentionally* allow Snolan to be seen. The boy felt unappreciated for all he had done; besides he set out to save Adria, and that was precisely what he accomplished.

The door to Adria's room was half ajar as Griffin approached it. Knocking lightly on it, he waited for her reply. "Come in," came a soft voice from the other side. Griffin pushed the rest of the door open and saw Adria sitting on her bed, sketching in her journal. Her hair was all pulled back behind her ears and out of her face as she had a wooden sketching utensil in hand. She tilted her face up from her busy work and saw Griffin standing in the doorway. Hurriedly, she placed the notebook to the side and crossed her arms. "You know, every time I worry you will not return...you always do." Her smile drew Griffin closer to her.

"Well, I guess you better stop worrying then," he slyly countered.

Griffin took Adria in his arms and hugged her with an intensity he was even surprised at. Seeing her well was *worth* every risk he took.

Griffin and Adria conversed well into the evening, catching up with one another. Even though they had only been apart for a few days, to them, it seemed like months. Their bond was an unbreakable chain. And even though they loved their Critin family, neither one of them could be in Aranwea without the other. They realized they were the only two humans in the land of Aranwea; however, this did not seem to concern either of them in the slightest degree.

"Snolan attacked a cop car!" Adria exclaimed as Griffin told her of their escape.

Griffin chuckled to himself as he tried to get the words out. "Yes! It was unbelievable!" Then Griffin paused for a moment. He scratched the back of his head as he continued, "Except...Snolan was seen, Adria."

Adria drew her face back as concern fell upon her. "Does Sable know?" she questioned.

"Yes," Griffin reluctantly replied, "and let me tell you, he is not happy about it."

"Well, of course he isn't, Griffin. They will surely be looking for her. And if this land is found, there will be a whole lot more to worry about than just the Shriekian."

Griffin could feel the frustration rising again within him. "Adria, I did not do this on purpose! It was the only way."

Adria placed her hand on his back and said, "I know, Griffin. I'm sorry. Everything will find its place, okay? Sable will come around, and we'll get this all sorted out."

Griffin, who had his face buried in his hands, shook his head lightly up and down. He stood up from her bedside and stated, "I'm going to clean up and get some rest, Adria."

She smiled to him and nodded her head. Nearly making his way out of the door, Adria spoke. "Griffin?" He spun around to face her once more. "Thank you..."

The boy blushed as an involuntary smile evolved on his face. Griffin looked to the ground then back to her and replied, "Glad to see you are better, Adria. Sleep well." Griffin shut the door lightly behind him and made his way toward his room.

As Griffin cleaned himself up from the prior events, he could see the scars that rested on his body. As he scanned his figure, the boy ran his hand down his stomach where one of the eels in the Shriekian domain had stung him. Griffin shuddered at the memories of being with the Shriekian. He evoked the hours spent in that prison, hoping and longing to be returned to the Critins. He remembered the escape and how the encounter with the Shriekian eggs nearly caused him to drown beneath the water. Brushing these thoughts to the side, Griffin slipped into his nighttime attire and got into bed. He gently blew out the candle that rested next to his bedside and then sunk his head down on the pillow. Placing his hands under his head, he stared up at the ceiling until his eyes grew heavy and sleep overcame him. Although the restless boy found sleep, his dreams were anything but normal.

Griffin tossed and turned in the night as his active mind swept him away like a fallen leaf on an endless river. He found himself in a large meadow, similar to the fields that filled the land of Aranwea. Even though it appeared to be familiar, Griffin did not know *exactly* where he was. As the dream continued, the boy walked around the green hills. He was by himself but did not feel alone. Griffin sensed as though something was guiding him, although he did not know what. All else was hazy around him, except for the green pasture before him. And then a voice came to him. It seemed as though it was many miles away, and Griffin could not make out what this mysterious voice was trying to say.

Cupping his hands around his lips, Griffin shouted, "*Helllllllo! Is anybody there?*" His words echoed throughout the area. And again, Griffin could hear a voice trying to make itself known to him; this time, it was a bit louder. And then the boy began to run in the direction of where he assumed the sounds were coming from. He raced up and down the steep hills as his lungs did not seem to tire. Now gaining more speed and covering more ground with every step, the words were clearer.

The voice was assertive, however, soothing as it spoke, "Go back to where your ancestors dwelled. There are more secrets that have been withheld."

Griffin stopped running as the words ended. He gazed about the sky and all around him to see where the voice was coming from. It seemed as though the voice was not coming from any particular direction; instead it was an overcast shadow that Griffin could not escape even if he desired to.

"Who's there?" he yelled. "What secrets?"

"Griffin."

Griffin spun around and saw what his eyes could not fathom. It was Eden. The creature stood before him on all fours. Its paws placed firmly on the ground, and it wings placed to the sides. His lion tail swished back and forth lightly as its white eyes locked onto Griffin's blue ones.

"Eden...?" the boy gasped as he took a step closer to the mighty griffin. "But...but this is impossible," he stuttered. "You are gone...you disappeared before my eyes!"

The creature's large beak extended into a smile as he said, "This is correct, my grandson. But it does not mean I have not been watching over you." The being paused as he extended his feathered neck behind him. Griffin looked to see what had caught the animal's attention. Darkness was consuming the fields directly behind them where Griffin had just had run from.

"What...what is *that*?" Griffin questioned.

"We do not have much time," the being replied. "My time with you is limited, even in your deepest dream, my dear boy."

"No," Griffin stated. "Why does it have to be like this?"

"Why is the sky infinite? Why do the rivers flow or the mountain terrains perish with time? It is the way things are, Griffin." Eden looked behind himself yet again as the darkness was creeping in closer, taking away all light that shone down on the green hills. It was an unavoidable shadow. "Now I have called upon some aid to offer you."

"Aid?" Griffin squinted his eyes as he tried to comprehend what Eden was making known to him.

"Yes. There is a great war coming, Griffin. It is a war that will dishonor all others. They will approach your castle and take what they need if you cannot acquire help with haste."

The shadow was now rapidly approaching as Griffin got out the words. "Wait, but who? Who can come to our aid? Where will I find them?"

"Go back to where your ancestors dwelled, my boy. There your rightful help shall be."

The blackness was now but twenty yards from them as Griffin panicked, "What do you mean? The altar? And I still cannot figure out the riddle, Eden!" Griffin was speaking of the riddle that he had been told when Griffin found Eden atop the mountain at the altar. "I must grasp it and not let it glow!"

The shadow was now touching the tip of the creature's tail as it moved in closer. Eden spoke his last words to Griffin, "Griffin, that answer can only be uncovered in your most desperate time of need." And before Griffin could respond, the blackness overcame Eden. The boy covered his head and crouched over as the darkness consumed him as well.

Griffin awoke in his bed, chest pounding and sweat glistening from his skin. He sat up abruptly, pulling the covers off of his heated body. He did not know what this dream meant to him, nor did he understand if it was his visions guiding him. All he knew was that this was all he had to go off of, and if there was truly a war approaching them, they needed to act quickly.

"Dream?" Adria asked with her hands on either side of her hips, eyebrows squinted downward in apprehension.

"Yes!" Griffin replied. "Adria, it was so real! I saw him—I saw Eden!" Griffin had found Adria in the morning's sunlight just outside the Critin village. She had not spent much time outside the castle due to her necessity to recover and had longed to feel the rays of sun on her skin like a warm, comforting blanket. "He told me that war was coming, a war to put all others to shame. Adria..." And then he paused for a moment. "I think this is it...after this, it will either be Shriekian in this land...or our Critin family...not both."

Adria's confused expression soon drained from her face as concern flooded her every emotion. She took a step back from Griffin, not making eye contact with him while nervously fiddling with her hands. "But...how do you know this was not just a *dream?* You can't be certain this was a vision, Griffin."

As a smile crept across his face the boy assured, "Adria, Eden is my grandfather. Even in my dreams, he would not leave me astray."

As she comprehended his words, Griffin waited for her reply. He knew that Adria could not fully grasp all that he was telling her. He knew that it would be a long shot trusting in this vision that came to him, but deep down in this boy, where no one else knew Griffin, he knew he must take this chance. "Well..."

she said. Griffin jerked his head up. "When are we leaving?"

Griffin quickly looked from left to right as uneasiness overcame him. He ran his fingers through his hair and down his neck as he said, "Adria, I am sorry, but you are still recovering and—"

Before Griffin could get another word out, she marched up to him clasped the palm of her hand across his active mouth. "No, no, no, no, Griffin Dominic! You're not leaving me out of this one. I feel perfectly well. I am coming with you, and that is that."

The boy knew once Adria's mind was set, there was no defying it. He rolled his eyes and lightly pushed her hand away from his mouth. He sighed. "Let's go talk to, Sable."

The two of them notified Sable of the dream that Griffin had. They told the diamond bearer of the assistance that was promised to them if they took this chance.

"War?" Sable's catlike eyes drew nearer as his senses heighted.

"Yes, Sable." Griffin needed him to understand.

The feathered being walked over to Griffin, placing his talon upon his shoulder, and declared, "If you think this is what is yet to come, my dear boy, it must be done."

TAKING ACTION

As Adria and Griffin prepared themselves for flight, thoughts raced through Adria's mind. *What if he is wrong? What if something happens while we are gone?* Griffin had a few worries of his own racing through his mind faster than he brain could process. He wondered, *What is this aid that Eden is speaking of? Can there truly be more help out there for us?*

Even though these questions passed through them, they did not voice them to each other. Both Adria and Griffin knew what was to come; they knew that an end was coming. That end was going to be the nonexistence of either race; Adria and Griffin just prayed it was not the end of them and the Critin family.

They packed light. Not bringing much more with them than a canteen of water and a meager amount of food. Griffin had his shortbow at his hands and his quiver on his back as Adria and Griffin waited Snolan's arrival atop the Oval. "Are you sure you're feeling up to this, Adria?" Griffin suspected.

Adria rolled her eyes in a sarcastic fashion and replied, "Yes, Griffin. I am not as helpless as you think I am."

Snolan arose from the side of the castle, her wings lightly casting up and down until she was at their side. Snolan knelt down as they climbed upon her back. They took flight into the midmorning air toward the mountainous terrain they had visited months prior. The air was chilly as Snolan seemed to be working effortlessly. Tilting her head back slightly, she directed her words toward Griffin, "What is all this talk about aid? There is no other kind here in Aranwea, Griffin..."

Griffin knew that her words seemed to be reliable, and if he was wrong—and if while they were away something happened to the

Critins—it would be all of his doing. Once again, the Critins' fate was resting on Griffin's shoulders. "I just know this is what we should be doing, Snolan."

"I trust you, Griffin," the dragon spoke.

"As do I," Adria added, her legs wrapped tightly around Snolan's belly and her arms tucked around Griffin. From the back of the airborne dragon, Adria gaped at the land beneath them.

This land of Aranwea was unlike any human could imagine. The only two humans who had ever got to witness such a pristine world was Adria and Griffin. Here in Aranwea, there wasn't the intoxicating smell of a car's exhaust pipe or the smog from plantations and mills mucking up the air. Here the trees were vast, with thick healthy roots that didn't have to worry about being unearthed. Here in Aranwea, the rivers were pure and could be drunk upon by any passerby without them questioning its wholesomeness. This land was truly and undeniably untouched, untouched in all means, except for the murky Shriekian domain, that is.

It wasn't a concern that this land would someday contain large skyscrapers that took over the forests. That was not a factor here. It was a different worry that was to be had in Aranwea. It was the worry that the Shriekian would make it their own. If the Shriekian had their way with the Critins, this flawless ground would be engulfed in marshland. The forests would be no more, and the clear creeks that ran through the Critin village would no longer to be pure. But instead, the entire land would be covered in *their* eroding waters. Smog of a different kind would bubble to the green surface of the waters, as sludge would wash upon the small parts of the dry land. Griffin and Adria knew that this could be the inescapable truth if they did not only act now but succeed as well in doing their actions. This was the eerie stillness before the great battle. If they wanted these lands to remain as it was now, they must find aid.

The three of them could see the huge mountain ahead. It looked a bit different due to the fact the seasons had changed since they were last there. The trees were vibrant in color and still took over most of the mountain. There were two things that had familiarity about it: the same clouds that hid the tip of the mountain were present and the clearing where they had landed before.

"You found it!" Griffin shouted, patting Snolan's white scales with his hand.

Snolan grinned, showing off her many pointed teeth as she said, "I never forget a place! You forget I used to come here many, many days ago to search for my lost family."

They flew toward the clearing. Snolan's wings tilted downward, enabling them to position themselves properly for landing. She touched down on the soil of the clearing on the mountain. The two boulders from before were still in place. The moss that was once upon them had dried out in the summer's heat.

Griffin spotted the two enlarged boulders and stated, "All right, it is this way!"

Before Adria and Griffin made their way up the slanted mountain, Snolan asked, "You have my whistle, correct?"

Adria lightly patted on the sack that was slung around her shoulder and assured, "Yep, it is right here, Snolan."

Snolan nodded her scaly head lightly and expressed, "Call on me if anything arises." The dragon then began to work her wings, causing the brush around them to move about and Adria's hair to spin around her face. Griffin and Adria watched her departure.

The boy then turned to Adria and held out his hand, "You ready for this?"

She lightly smiled and took his hand in hers. They made their way in between the boulders and into the woods before them. The trek was not an excruciating exertion of their energy; however it was not the easiest climb, either. Along the way, they found a fallen redwood tree in their path. The trunk of it was mammoth as it came up to their hips where the two of them stood. Being that it would take much longer to go around the tree, they decided to go over it.

Adria placed her hands atop the ridged bark and hoisted herself up. Standing on the collapsed redwood, she stared down the entire tree's length. "Wow," she gasped, "this tree is never ending, Griffin!"

Griffin soon joined her. Brushing off some tree particles that had brushed up against him, he saw what had Adria in amazement. He squinted his vibrant eyes and slowly raised his head upward as he followed the infinite trunk. He shifted his head toward Adria and hastily ran his fingers through his messy hair.

Griffin gasped. "What...what could have done this?"

Adria did not answer; instead, she was turned in the opposite direction of the boy, eyeing at the path they had ahead.

Griffin turned his head to the side. "Ummm...A...Adria? What is it?"

"That." She pointed her finger ahead. Griffin turned to where she was motioning. As they stood atop, they saw a sea of fallen trees trailing the one they were standing on. "What *is* this, Griffin?"

Griffin stood motionless next to her for a few moments, then said, "I don't know, Adria. But this? This is not normal."

The two of them slid off the tree trunk and made their way on the path where the numerous redwoods lay unearthed before them.

Over an hour went by, Adria and Griffin's hands were sticky with pitch and bark. Their clothes were brown with dirt stains, and their hair had twigs all about them. As they lifted themselves over the last tree that was in their path, they pushed through some brush that was before them, and on the other side was the oversized stairs that led to the cave where Griffin found Eden.

SCALES

Adria and Griffin approached the entrance to the cave with caution. After hurling themselves over the collapsed redwoods, what would be next was unknown. Walking through the tunnel, it was just as Griffin recollected. It was not the same as the cave that had led him into Aranwea. This one was different. It was dry and cool. The stone that made up the cavern was a light shade of gray and did not possess jagged stalagmites and stalactites around it. There were no loose soil or rocks beneath their feet as they went along, either. Instead, it had smooth flooring, with a rounded ceiling above them. Although the appearance of the cave was the same as before, there was something that was distinctively different. As Griffin and Adria went along the way, the light from outside the tunnel was slowly fading, disrupting their vision.

Griffin took his shortbow off of his shoulder. He grasped it in his hand as he and Adria moved deeper. "I do not understand," he worded.

As the light continued to leave their presence, their steps grew slower and shorter.

"What's wrong, Griffin?" Adria asked as she strolled next to the boy, keeping her pace in sync with his.

"I do not remember it being this dark."

As soon as Griffin muttered these words, the light that was emitted from behind them vanished completely. Adria and Griffin jolted their bodies around to see as to why the light from the outside had left their presence in such an instant. But they could see nothing.

"What is going on!?" Griffin shouted. His voice echoed throughout the place, and his words bounced off the walls, allowing them to hear his words long after they were spoken. It was as if a great storm had broken all electrical currents and left them to the darkness, although this could not be the case here.

"Griffin!" Adria panicked. She blindly swatted her arms around to find where the boy stood.

"I'm here, Adria!" He found her side and brought himself closer to her.

The pitch-black surrounding controlled and consumed every essence of their being. Neither of them could see their hand before their face or the next step their feet would take.

"Just-just stay next to me!" Griffin bellowed. Again his words bounced off the sightless walls. Adria held onto Griffin's t-shirt so she would not be separated. The boy blindly reached for his quiver. His hand was shaking as he found an arrow. Griffin brought it to the front of him, and found the bow's stringing. He pulled back on the cord, getting ready to release the pointed arrow at whatever stood in their way. Although, this did not do much good, considering he could not see anything to shoot at even if he desired it.

Adria tugged at his shirt, her heart racing with anxiety, and she slowly started to pull him backward. "Let's just backtrack out of here, Griffin!" She panicked. The frightened girl continued to try and pull him back to where she thought they had just come from, but Griffin did not move. "C'mon!" She was now shouting as fear crept even further inside of her, making its way to the center of her soul.

"Adria!" he countered, taking the arrow off of its stringing. "There is a reason why there is no more light here...we can't just backtrack!" Griffin took in a deep breath while trying to calm his own nerves. "The entrance is shut..."

These words terrified Adria as her hands began to shake. "No...why would the entrance close!" She was losing her wits, and Griffin could surely recognize this. Holding his bow and putting the arrow away, he wrapped his arm around her body.

Griffin held her tightly under his arm as still no sign of light was revealed. They felt trapped, alone, and entirely immersed in the cave's shadows. And as Griffin and Adria shuddered in their dismay, a loud, uninviting sound came from what proclaimed to be across the cave. It was a long-drawn-out rumble that started from the end of the tunnel and echoed down, making its way to where Adria and Griffin helplessly stood.

"G...Griffin..." Adria whispered.

"I know...I heard it too." Griffin withdrew his arm from Adria's shoulder and draped his shortbow around his own shoulder. Finding the straps on his quiver, he quickly tugged at them, tightening them closer to his body. Feeling for Adria, he wrapped his fingers firmly around her wrist. "Maybe we *should* try and backtrack a little," the boy stated as the rumbling started up again. They could hear it getting closer as it sounded like an unpleasant cry of a mother bear protecting its cubs. "*Now!*" Griffin shouted. He yanked on Adria's arms as they began to quickly walk backward.

The noise was growing immensely, and they could now feel the ground shaking and hear snarls echoing throughout the premises.

"I cannot see where we are going, Griffin!" Adria screamed as they turned their bodies around completely to pick up their pace in the direction in which they came from.

"Just follow me!" the boy reassured with his fingers still closed around her wrist. Griffin and Adria were at a slow jog now as Griffin kept his free hand in front of his body so they would not collide with the cavern walls. The growling was continuing to pursue them when Griffin shouted, "There has to be another way...!" And then the boy stopped in his tracks all together for his hand ran into something before them. Adria, not able to react to Griffin's sudden standstill, ran into the back of him, causing Griffin to completely crash into the object that was before him. As Griffin's body crashed into the unknown entity, he could feel one thing, and one thing only, as he collided—scales.

LET THERE BE LIGHT

Griffin's body bounced off of the mysterious being and stumbled backward into Adria in the dark. "Who...whose there!" Griffin demanded.

Adria, now practically holding Griffin up in her arms, countered, "Why are you falling into me?"

The grumbling from behind them was now clearer than ever as they could hear it nearing them.

Regaining his balance, he stood next to her and whispered, "Back up, Adria...now."

"I'm starting to question your sanity, Griffin! Do you not hear what is coming behind us?" She began to increasingly shove him forward as he resisted her, trying to push her backward.

"I don't think you realize what I just ran into, Adria!"

The two of them pushed each other back and forth for a few moments longer until something occurred that allowed them to see the room in which they stood. Flames began to reveal themselves, starting on the other side of the cave. The sides of the cavernous walls started to emit fire from hundreds of black torches positioned into them. They were lit one by one, each following another in the inferno. As soon as a torch was lit, the other next to it would set to fire as well. Adria and Griffin watched the flames in awe, as the light in the room was growing stronger with every second.

"*Why are you in this cavern?*" came a powerful voice from behind.

Griffin, being mesmerized by the flames had completely forgotten what he had run into. The two of them spun around to see who had spoken these forceful words, and when they did, their eyes were affixed onto a being they had never believed to exist. It was a crimson dragon. Her sturdy wings were tucked to the side of her body. She possessed two horns protruding from her scale-covered head.

Griffin observed the dragon's black spikes, which trailed from the top of her long neck all the way down to the tip of her tail. These spikes looked ever so familiar to the boy. "My dream!" he gasped, eyes widening and heart skipping beats.

Adria stood immobile and completely frozen where she stood. She quickly glanced back to see if there were any other beings coming from the direction they were hearing the deafening roars.

The dragon bared her jagged teeth and took a step toward Adria and Griffin, planting her four feet to the ground just a meager foot or two away from them. She roared, "*Will you not answer me!*"

Griffin, recalling Eden's words, explained, "We have come to find aid. There is a great war coming."

The dragon then began to slowly circle Griffin and Adria, sniffing at them with her enlarged nostrils as she made her rounds. "You come from Critin grounds."

"Yes, yes, we do! We mean no harm. We just need assistance. It is the Shriekian. There is a great war—"

And before Griffin could mouth another sentence, the dragon snarled, "Shriekian you said?"

"Yes. They are getting stronger. We need your help!" Griffin clenched his fist tightly, hoping and praying this was in fact the aid that Eden had spoken of. The boy knew that the lost dragon race could be of vital help to them if they could convince their assistance.

"There is no aid to be had here." She then stopped circling them and glared at Adria and Griffin, her yellow eyes showing no mercy.

"But that is why we are here!" Adria began. "That is why you are here, and we found you! Can't you see that—"

The red dragon blew some air out of her nostrils and slowly tossed her hefty face from side to side. "That is where you are wrong, young human. We were summoned here by some outside being. But there is nothing for us here!"

"Eden..." Griffin whispered to Adria.

"We have been in search of the leader of our lost dragon race for many decades now. But they are nowhere to be found. I feel our efforts and this travel has been purposeless."

"Why is your race lost...what happened?" Adria was now pressing the questions. She thought if she could understand the dragon and comprehend what it was exactly that happened to them, she could convince them to help.

Her yellow eyes locked onto Adria's. "What happened to *my* kind? The same thing that is about to happen to the Critins. The Shriekian."

Adria's emotions began to arise. Griffin intercepted her body language. Adria's fist clenched and teeth tightened as she began to conjure her next words. Griffin said in a hushed tone, "Adria, don't...just let it be for now."

Just as Griffin supposed this, Adria ignored his warning and spoke harshly, "You are nothing but a coward! Don't you want vengeance on the Shriekian! They nearly wiped your kind from existence, and you have no remorse that they are about to do this again...to another kind!"

The now exceedingly angry dragon took a large step toward Adria. The beast's nose was but a few inches from her face as Adria did not move one muscle. Instead, she stared into the dragon's eyes, showing her that intimidation was not a factor here. Adria could feel the warm air from the dragon's mouth as she heavily breathed into her face. "How do you know of this?" the dragon asked.

Griffin, who was witnessing the entire scene, nervously reached his arm out to Adria. He pulled her away from the heated being as he spoke, "Because there is another dragon. She is the castle guardian of the Critins! And she has been looking for you! You do not know what this will mean to her!"

The red dragon laughed a menacing tune, revealing her sharp teeth. As she finished her cackling, she regained herself finding the words. "There are no other dragons. Lies will not bring us to your side. We are a free race and shall not act until we are called upon by the leader of our kind."

Adria's eyes began to flash and slowly closed into slits. Nostrils flaring, she shouted, "There *is* another dragon! And her name is Snolan! I guess she got the valiant characteristics of a dragon! Bravery, loyalty, and strength in all aspects... something you obviously did not obtain!"

"*Adria!*" Griffin panicked.

The dragon's jaw snapped shut, making a deafening cracking sound. Griffin quickly stepped in front of Adria as the dragon attempted to pursue her.

"I suggest you leave this cave. *Immediately!*" The dragon bellowed an outstanding roar down the entire cave, causing Adria and Griffin's ears to ring with pain. As soon as the sound subsided, the entrance to the outside reopened and all flames around them dissolved into the air.

"Please," Griffin started, "Adria did not mean to speak so harshly. Please forgive her."

"I do *not* need you to apologize for me, Griffin Dominic!" Adria resented.

Trying to keep her behind him where the dragon could not see her, he shadowed her movement as Adria tried to get around him. "We are just in such desperate need of help. And that is why we speak the way we do...please I can prove to you there is another dragon! I can prove it all!"

"No one was there when the Shriekian slaughtered *my* kind. Had there been more of us, it would not have been a problem." She shuddered as she envisioned the attack. "Our flames were not strong enough..." Getting lost in her thoughts, the being hastily jolted her head to the side, brushing away the wretched memories. "I am sorry, but there is no help to be had here." The being then shifted her body in the other direction and started to leave Adria and Griffin. "Please leave."

Griffin started his way toward the exit, and Adria did not follow. She flung her hands in the air and contorted her face in an expression of disapproval. "So that's it, Griffin? She, and the rest of the lost dragon race, is our only chance of beating them!"

Griffin stopped and turned back to her. "Adria, did you not hear her words? There is no convincing them!"

"Well, maybe Snolan can! We can't just let this pass us by! Your vision brought us here for a reason. Eden summoned us *and* the dragons here for a reason!"

Griffin knew she spoke the truth. But something in his gut told him that right now, he just needed to get back to the Critins. "C'mon." He signaled her to follow with his arm. "Let's call on Snolan. She will know what to do." Griffin turned in the other direction as he picked up his pace.

"What's the hurry?" she questioned as she started to jog to meet back up with him.

"Something is not right."

"With the Critins?"

"Yes."

A NEW KIND OF FLIGHT

As they made their way down the stairs that led them into the cave, Adria took the whistle out of the knapsack that draped across her shoulders. Taking the wooden instrument in her hand, she pressed the tip of the whistle to her lips and sent a lungful of air through it. Griffin clasped his hands over his ears as the falsetto was released. As the sound subsided, Griffin took his hands off his ears. Using his right arm as a visor, he gazed into the sky for any sign of Snolan. Adria did the same as they stood in silence awaiting her arrival.

But she did not come. The distraught boy shifted his body in every direction, causing the quiver on his back to swing from side to side. "Where do you think she is?" Griffin questioned.

Adria, lost in contemplation, did not think to respond to what was being asked of her. She continued to stare off into the sky, eyes wide with apprehension and stomach turning in knots as each moment passed without any sign of their friend.

"Adria!" Griffin shouted.

Startled, she jumped backward and shifted her now irritated eyes at Griffin. She retorted, "I do not know where she is, Griffin!"

Minutes passed, and still there was no glimpse of the airborne dragon; Griffin began to grow desperate. The boy hastily flung his quiver to one side of him and dropped it to the soil. He then took the shortbow off his other arm and set it to the ground.

"Easy, Griffin!" Adria spoke firmly as she observed the boy disregarding his belongings.

"Keep calling on her, Adria." Griffin then cupped his two hands around his mouth, making a funnel. Tilting his face upward, he started to bellow, "Snolaaaaaaan!"

Adria did as Griffin suggested and continued to drive air from her chest into the whistle. The mixture of Griffin's voice and the whistle made quite a commotion throughout Aranwea. Only a few minutes passed since they began their eager endeavor to bring Snolan to them when they saw something flying toward their area in the distance. Griffin subsided his words, and Adria took the whistle from her lips. "Look, Griffin!" Adria paraded up and down and pointed to the object coming their way. "She is coming!"

"It worked, Adria! It worked!" he answered making his way toward her with open arms. Adria embraced him in a hug as they watched the entity coming their way. "We are here!" Griffin shouted, one arm still wrapped around Adria's shoulder and the other waved back and forth in the air.

As the mysterious object came closer, Adria squinted her eyes in disbelief and her smile swept from her face, like a meager fishing boat on an angry sea. "Griffin..." Her words did not come easy. "That is not Snolan."

Griffin eyebrows drew closer together as he took a step in front of her. "Huh?" He gasped. The two of them could see that what was coming toward them was not one large being; it was four smaller beings flying toward them. "Adria, you are right! That isn't Snolan." Griffin paused a moment, still studying the sky. "Those are Critins!"

"Critins?"

"Yes! What are they doing?" Griffin held his hands and arms out in front of himself and shrugged his shoulders in puzzlement. Griffin then began to holler in the direction of the Critins' flight and waved his arms up and down. "Over here! Over here!" the boy repeated.

The four Critins touched down to the earth in which the two of them stood. Each of the beings feathers was greatly ruffled as they tried to regain air into their lungs. They all contained bands around their lower halves of their bodies that owned two daggers that were securely placed in slots on either side of them.

"What is going on? Where is Snolan?" Griffin could feel his adrenaline coursing through his veins as the hairs on his arms began to stand on edge.

They continued to inhale great amounts of oxygen until the one named Lisal exasperated, "We must leave...now!" Griffin raced over to his fallen shortbow and quiver and secured them about his body once more.

"Why?" Adria moved closer to one of the Critins. "Where is Snolan?"

"Snolan could not be here! It is the Shriekian...at the castle!" The Critin was finally regaining her senses. "Snolan did her best to direct us here, but we got misguided until we heard the whistle again and Snolan's name being called upon. Snolan could not leave the castle grounds. She is keeping them out!"

"And how do you propose we get back without, Snolan!" Adria was speaking bitterly.

Lisal, who was doing the majority of the speaking, nodded her feathered face to the other three. They all took flight into the air above after her command. Lisal remarked, "You seem to have underestimated the strength of us Critins." She then began to work her wings in an upward fashion until her talons left the soil, and she joined the other three in the air. And like a birds of prey stalking their next meal, they swooped down to where Griffin and Adria stood motionless.

"Hold your arms outward!" one of them hollered. Adria and Griffin reluctantly looked toward each other and then did as they were told. As this happened, one Critin clasped its talon precisely around Griffin's right arm as another retrieved the left. The remaining two accomplished the same act to Adria, and with a quick tug, the two of them were lifted off the ground and headed back to the Critin Castle where much awaited them.

FIGHT FOR OUR EXISTENCE

"This is no ending my good Critins!"

Vetch stood at the basin of the castle with all warriors lined up behind him. The first wave of the Shriekian soldiers had already hit the castle. The Critin army was able to fend them off, but this was not without a cost. Nearly fifty Critins had fallen in this act, and this was just the beginning of a battle that would be in the remembrance of Aranwea for all eternity.

"We shall not back down!" Vetch roared so all could hear.

The Critin soldiers raised their bows and daggers to the air and released a battle cry that could be heard for miles to come.

Vetch strutted up and down the line to where all awaited his command. "We Critins have something that the Shriekian do not! We contain bravery buried deep beneath our feathers! The passion we withhold for our own kind shall outshine the darkest shadows! It shall drink dry the murkiest depths! And shall fly higher than any star could ever fathom!" Vetch paused for a moment. "We shall fight for our existence!"

The soldiers grew quiet as the leader spoke, taking in every ounce of inspiration. They were focused, determined, and, most of all, completely absorbed in what was yet to come. The soldiers' catlike eyes drew closer together as their grip on their bows grew tighter.

Emerging from over the hillside, just before the beginning of the pathway of the Critin village, was a crawling creature. It was a Shriekian. It stood on top of the hill before them, many yards away. Its slimy legs dripped with sludge, and an enlarged mouth oozed green saliva. Something about this creature made it different than the usual Shriekian. This creature had one eye open, and the other, where an eye should be, was one gaping hole. It was Wretch, the creature Griffin wounded when escaping the Shriekian domain. It was motionless, staring with its one eye directly at Vetch.

"Hold your ground!" Vetch bellowed to all.

The Critin army did as he commanded. The lone Shriekian started to trudge down the hillside and, in doing so, left a trail of grungy substance. It stopped about halfway down the green pasture and, without moving an inch further, released an earsplitting roar from its wretched mouth. Soon after the howl subsided, shadows of beasts began to appear from behind the creature. He had called upon the army. Hundreds of beasts lined up atop the hill, waiting for *their* next command. It was a sea of destruction as their alien-like eyes were fixed upon the Critin castle. The Shriekian army was teeming with energy as one of them snapped to the leader, "What are we waiting for!"

The one-eyed being remarked, "We wait for Gotham's command!"

Adria and Griffin could now see the castle before them as the four Critins exhausted every ounce of energy they had within them to bring them to the castle grounds.

"Look!" Griffin gasped, his arm outstretched and pointing toward the basin of the castle.

Adria acknowledged Griffin's statement; however, her eyes were being entertained by something else. "There are so many of them..."

"I know!" Griffin smiled as he gazed down below. "Look at all our soldiers!"

"No, Griffin. Look..." Adria raised her hand and pointed in the direction of the hill.

And then Griffin realized what she meant as his eyes fell upon the hundreds of Shriekian soldiers. "How...?" he asked as the four Critins plummeted to the basin of the castle where Vetch stood commanding the army. Images of the Shriekian eggs Griffin came across when escaping their waters reentered his mind. *Why didn't I destroy those when I saw them? There are so many of them*, he pondered to himself. Hurriedly, he shook these thoughts out of his mind as he acknowledged there was much more to worry about now in the present. The four Critins who were carrying the two of them eased themselves downward and set them to the ground before Vetch.

"My friends," Vetch spoke as he moved closer to Griffin, slinging his sack of arrows to one side of him. "Did you find the aid that you were in search of?" The Critin's eyes widened with faith and hopefulness. Griffin did not look at Vetch directly, and the hope that the creature once held was swept from his scarred face. "Well...then we shall fight until we can no more."

The crowd of soldiers behind them began to part, and stepping through was another Critin with a vivid color of red hanging about his neck. It was Sable. The diamond bearer looked at Griffin and Adria. Before a word could be released, there came a deafening growl that neither Critin nor human had ever heard in their days. It came from the direction where the enemy positioned themselves.

Emerging overhead, flying from behind the entire Shriekian army, was a shadow much larger than any other mortal in Aranwea. The silhouette owned expanded black bat-like wings that gently flapped in an up-and-down motion, propelling the rest of its body forward. Its body was covered with thick black scales, making it the ideal defense mechanism. And from the tip of the prehistoric being's sturdy tail to the top of its head and two sharp horns were sharp spikes. Its two eyes were a deep red, which had black slits down the middle like a venomous serpent.

It was Gotham, the leader of all Shriekians—and Snolan's only brother. As soon as the mighty dragon passed the top of the green hill where the enemy line rested, all Shriekians began to follow his flight and moved closer to the Critin castle. Gotham was a great distance in front of the rest as he hurled his body toward the Critin army, snarling and showing off his enlarged fangs.

"*Front lines, fire!*" Vetch turned to his army and bellowed. "Back lines, take flight!" The soldiers did as they were told as the first four rows all took an arrow in hand and directed it at the dragon coming their way. They set the arrows free as Gotham continued his relentless pursuit. Each arrow did impact him; however, his scale-consumed body protected him. His body was a mighty shield and offered no consequence.

The other Critins who took flight after Vetch's command attempted to fly in wide circles around the vile dragon. They did this for Gotham was not their target. These soldiers' quest was to bring down as many Shriekian soldiers as they could before they reached the castle. As the beings attempted to make their way through the air around Gotham, the dragon intercepted their intentions and released a deadly inferno from his jaws. "*Flames!*" one of them shouted as they witnessed Gotham's fire.

Many of the soldiers were able to dodge the combustions; however, some did not as their wings were set to fire and they were forced to plummet to the ground in a downward spiral. Gotham was now closing in on the army that was grounded as the remaining soldiers continued to fire arrow upon arrow on his powerful physique. Each arrow deflected off of him as if a metal force field was engulfing his body.

Gotham was now but forty yards from the basin of the castle as he puffed his mouth to full length and conjured an unfathomable fiery wrath deep within his lungs. Griffin and Adria stood before the army as the dragon came closer with every moment. Griffin ripped an arrow from his quiver and set it at his strings. He hastily pointed the arrow directly at the right eye of the black dragon. Just as Gotham was about to set free another blazing fire, a forceful being came hurling through the air at him, striking him directly in the side, causing him to unwillingly release the fire up into the air and away from the castle.

Griffin lowered his shortbow as he witnessed Gotham being brought down from the air from no one other than Snolan. As Snolan struck him, they crashed into the village huts, causing the stone that held them together to crumble to the ground. As the dust subsided, Gotham made it to his all fours. Snolan lay a few yards from him, bleeding from one of her mangled claws. She slowly brought herself to her feet with much effort, and as she did, the dragon saw Gotham from afar with his head tilted downward in a menacing fashion and tail whipping from side to side.

"Ah, to what do I owe the pleasure?" The black dragon cackled. "My sister, still on the feeble side of the food chain, I see."

Snolan tossed her head from left to right, shaking off the loose debris. Moving closer to him with a slight limp in her step, she snapped, "I am no sister of yours, Gotham. I think we established that many, many years ago."

The two feuding dragons slowly began to circle one another. Loud clashing and snarls began to occur near the Critin castle. Snolan glanced to the side to see the Critins fighting to protect the grounds. The Shriekians had made their way to the front line as some Critins were flying from above, raining arrows upon their forsaken bodies; others were battling from the ground fighting with their daggers and talons. The Critins were undeniably outnumbered as nearly every single Critin soldier was battling gallantly as not even half the Shriekian army was even involved in the war. This was because the Shriekians did not need to exert their entire army just yet; instead, they stood behind their fighting soldiers, waiting their turn in line, their turn to attack.

Snolan and Gotham continued to circle one another like wildcats stalking their soon-to-be meal. Snolan attempted to show no pain from her already injured body as Gotham strutted firmly, holding his chest high in his boastful might.

"You see them." The dark dragon tossed his head arrogantly to the clashing beings at the castle basin. "*They* answer to me and me only. If you could be so kind to hand me over the diamond bearer *and* the boy, I shall spare your sorrowful life, my sister. As for the Critins, I am sorry, but they must be abolished."

Snolan's ocean blue eyes turned into small slits as she lowered her head. Snorting a short burst of air through her nostrils in disapproval, she yelled, "*Neither* of those testimonies are even vaguely an option."

Gotham cackled loud and deeply within his throat once again revealing his powerful jaws. "Then you have chosen death as well."

"I know Shriekians and Critins can no longer share Aranwea, which is why the Shriekians shall be no more." She paused for a moment and then demanded, "But what could you possibly want with the boy!"

Gotham sunk his head downward and swayed it side to side as he countered, "Sometimes I cannot fathom that you and I are from the same kin! The boy and Adria are not from this world. And after I slaughter the Critin race, that boy *will* take me and my Shriekian kind to *his* world." Gotham then stopped in his tracks as Snolan did the same. "You know you cannot overpower me. When it came to genes, my sister, the stronger ones were given to me."

Gotham then turned his head to the sky, and stretching his neck to full length, he freed another boisterous roar from deep in his throat. All other Shriekians positioned behind the battle, which were yet to be involved, charged to the front lines. For every solitary Critin, there was at least three overpowering Shriekians.

"*Stop! Call them back!*" Snolan cried as she charged at the dark dragon.

Adria, who had acquired a bow from a fallen soldier, was fighting alongside Griffin. Her bow work had grown greatly as she brought them down, but even it was not enough. Three slimy creatures clasped their ghastly claws around her arms, detaining her. Griffin, who was dodging creatures hurling in his direction, saw Adria struggling with the animals.

"Get off of me!" Adria shouted as she thrashed her arms from side to side.

"Adria!" Griffin was trying to make his way to her as he pulled an arrow from his quiver and, using it as a knife, stabbed it into the beasts in his way. The boy saw Vetch to his side; he had two sharp knives in either hand. He was slashing the Shriekian soldiers left and right, bringing them down by the second. "Vetch," Griffin pleaded, "help Adria!"

Vetch glanced to where Adria struggled as a Shriekian came at him open jawed and teeth bared. The leader of the army swiftly retracted the dagger in his talon and thrust it deep into the mouth and through the throat of the creature. And in doing so, it caused one of the animal's teeth to sink into his arm. He roared with pain, and as Vetch pulled away from the suffering monster, its front fang remained protruding from his feathered arm. Vetch reached around with his other talon and gripped it tightly, ripping it from his bleeding limb. Vetch could feel the Shriekian venom spread through his veins as he turned back to Adria who was now being dragged away from the battle field. Freeing himself of two more enemies, and gripping onto his bloodied arm, he made his way to Adria.

"Back to the cage with you, Miss Adria!" One of them had their rubbery arm slung around her throat, causing Adria to gasp violently for air. The other two seized both of her arms. The creatures witnessed Vetch coming their way as they hurriedly pulled her away from the battle scene. Vetch swiftly opened his wings and swiped them downward with force; his legs left the ground as he launched himself in their direction. And with the blades in each of his hands he flew at them arms wide, approaching them from an aerial attack. Vetch swiftly circled around the Shriekians who were detaining Adria, and before the beast could react, he planted his talons to the ground and thrust both of the daggers into the back of the one choking her. Immediately, the being dropped to the soil as Vetch withdrew his blades.

"Release her!" Vetch stood strongly before Adria and the other two who held her. "Or I shall destroy you like your friend before me!"

The two Shriekians looked to the ground at their deceased soldier who was nothing but a lifeless corpse oozing a black liquid from its back. They hissed at Vetch and bared their treacherous fangs at him.

"Vetch! Behind you!" Adria cried.

As Vetch turned around to see what had her so distraught, five Shriekian soldiers brought him to the ground, smothering him beneath their slippery bodes. "Adria!" Vetch shouted as he failed to lift himself up from beneath the pile. Adria watched as the Shriekian creatures consumed him beneath their vile bodies.

The Critin army was diminishing by the second. The Shriekians had penetrated the castle and had found their way to the young Critins who were hiding desperately in the dungeon. The Shriekian army was too much for this race. The Critins had clung on to their existence for many decades now; however, they had barely kept their heads above water. And as the war waged on and more Critin blood was shed, Griffin stopped fighting all together. And in his state of delirium, he set his bow to the ground and slung his quiver off his back. Eyes half open and blood dripping from his lacerated jaw, he witnessed a fellow Critin soldier falling before him.

Griffin slowly knelt down next to the suffering creature, whose last breaths were near. It was Lisal, the Critin who had helped him get back to the castle not an hour prior. Her yellow beak was cracked in two places as one of her eyes was so severely swollen that she could not even open it. Griffin hovered above the wounded soldier on his knees before him. The Critin conjured enough strength as she lifted their talon toward Griffin's chest. Placing its hand over Griffin's heart, the boy wrapped his hand around the wrist of the being, holding it closer to him.

Griffin closed his blue florescent eyes as tears began to trickle down them. And as the tears continued and more Critins fell to the castle grounds before him, he softly sobbed, "I...I...I couldn't do enough..." Griffin placed his other hand beneath the head and horns of the feathered being before him and pressed the Critin's talon closer to his chest.

"Griffin..." the dying Critin spoke, "until the last standing soldier...there is hope." Griffin sunk his head down and began to sob in utter dismay, still clinging onto the creature's talon until it grew limp, announcing the death of it.

The side door at the basin of the castle sprung open. Fifty Shriekian soldiers marched out of the doorway. First to come out was Clythe. The enemy was not alone—not alone in even the slightest degree. It was a wretched nightmare as they trudged out of the castle doorway, each clutching onto a Critin youngster. Some were so small, so petite that it was as if they had been hatched not a few weeks prior. Their soft premature feathers were not golden brown like an adult Critin, and instead they were a light yellow. Many of the babies were wide eyed, with tears glistening down their small faces. The remaining Critin soldiers witnessed what was occurring and attempted to lunge toward the babies; however, the Shriekian army detained them in an instant.

"*Halt*, Shriekian army of Aranwea!" Clythe held his slimy claw upward while still controlling the baby Critin beneath him.

Griffin raised his head weakly and saw the Critin babies peering down to him. He saw every ounce of terror in their enlarged eyes.

The army did as they were commanded.

"Bring the remaining Critins to the center!"

The Shriekians circled around where Griffin still rested at his knees. The boy, at last, let go of the deceased Critin's talon before him as the remaining soldiers were being shoved toward the middle with him. The adversaries moved in closer, closing off any means of escaping their circle of terror. Griffin felt a familiar hand slip beneath his arm, supporting him so he could be brought to his feet. Griffin turned to around to see Adria before him. Her arms were deeply lacerated from where the Shriekians had constrained her. Her dark brown hair was tangled and matted as a bruise rested just beneath her left eye socket. She brought Griffin closer to her, helping support his body. The boy locked onto her green eyes with his blue ones as the last Critin soldiers, villagers, and babies of Aranwea surrounded them in the center of the teeming Shriekian army.

Griffin heaved in a great amount of oxygen from his depleted lungs, and lifting his hand, he brushed Adria's hair up and out of her face and behind her ear. "Adria..." The boy struggled to get the words out as he swallowed deeply. "I would have stayed in Aranwea with you... forever..."

In that instantaneous moment, Adria closed her eyes. And with all the death and destruction going on around them and the fallen family scattered about the castle grounds like discarded pieces of rubbish, Adria recollected each moment spent with Griffin. She recalled Griffin finding her at the Shriekian domain and being taught how to use a bow and arrow by Griffin. Adria remembered images of her and Griffin sitting beneath the comforting redwoods of Aranwea and conversing about their lives for hours at a time, learning and growing in admiration for one another. She evoked the way she felt when he was near and how she never *truly* felt alive until he came into her life.

As these memories subsided, she opened her eyes and saw the boy before her. And placing her hand around him, she brought him closer to her, slowly pressing her lips to his. Griffin wrapped his arms around Adria, and for that split second, all thoughts of the war around them evaporated as they held each other in powerful, captivating affection. All sounds from the weeping creatures escaped them. Every part of despair seemed to have disappeared as their lips pulled apart.

Adria and Griffin gazed at each other for another moment, and then bringing themselves back to reality, they looked to see why the enemies' circle was now parting down the middle. The boy intertwined his fingers in Adria's as they and the rest of the Critin family watched what was yet to come.

THE LAST RIDDLE

Coming through the threatening crowd was Snolan. She limped helplessly as a group of ten Shriekians escorted her to the middle. They snapped at her violently, forcing her to move faster even though her body would not allow it without causing her great pain. Her face was battered and swollen, while the tip of her left horn was missing. The once pure-white dragon now possessed claw markings along her belly and neck that seeped a darkened red. She made her way to the remaining Critins, Adria, and Griffin then collapsed to the ground, taking in shallow breaths. Snolan was defeated.

"Snolan!" Adria sobbed. Letting go of Griffin's hand, she ran to the dragon's side.

Emerging through the crowd was a large shadowy being that contained large bite marks around its body. Even though it appeared to be wounded, it walked with might and poise. Gotham had joined them. And in front of the vile beast was a glowing radiance of red. The dark dragon had one claw clasped around Sable as he restrained him and walked him to the middle where the rest of his Critin family was captured. Stepping out of the crowd of Critins was Mogol. His body was greatly mangled, and the sacks of dust that he usually had clinging about his belt were torn apart, containing no sand. He limped forward, making his way closer to the dragon and his dear friend Sable.

"Stop, Mogol!" Sable desperately demanded.

Gotham clenched down tighter his claws around Sable's small-feathered neck. "Silence!" the dragon boomed. "If the Critin wishes to come forth...let him." The dragon's scowl turned into a menacing smirk.

Mogol ceased his approach ten yards from where the dark dragon stood. Silence fell upon the scene as one could only hear the swift breeze rustling through the mighty redwoods and the soft trickle of the stream that flowed through the Critin village. Mogol closed his watery eyes.

Gotham cocked his head to one side and questioned, "What say you, Mogol?"

Mogol opened his eyes and looked at Sable. He gave him the look of departure, the look of a good-bye. It was a nonverbal notion, and Sable knew this. Mogol then positioned his face upward and spoke, "You have the diamond, Gotham. You have caused us greater suffering than you could ever fathom. Take the diamond, and release him. Let my Critins die in peace."

"Peace?" Gotham turned to Wretch and nodded his prehistoric head to him. "Let *me* show you peace, foolish dust keeper."

Wretch then rotated to call upon three more Shriekian soldiers. And as he did, they rapidly lunged toward Mogol. However, Mogol did not move; instead, he shut his weeping eyes and accepted his undeniable fate.

"*No!*" Sable bellowed as he attempted to spring toward Mogol.

Gotham clenched down tighter upon Sable's body, bringing him to the ground. And as this happened, the creatures brought down Mogol, mauling his weary body before the whole Critin family. All Shriekians snarled with satisfaction as this wretched act took place, lifting their slippery claws in the air with approval. Sable buried his face in his talons as he wept uncontrollably. When the beasts had dragged Mogol's deceased body off to the side, Sable looked up and saw his Critin family in utter horror.

"To your feet, diamond bearer!" Gotham commanded.

Sable struggled to his feet as the red gem dangled about his neck. He turned to face the dragon before him. Gotham towered over him as Sable stretched his neck to full length to look up to him. "The destruction of the diamond will put an end to our race, but our legacy will always be here in Aranwea," Sable stated as he began to lift the chain, which held the diamond off his neck.

"*Stop!*" Gotham boomed. Sable released the chain, allowing it to fall back around his chest. "Where is Griffin Dominic?"

All Shriekian and Critin eyes fell upon the boy. The boy's fists were clenched, his jaw tightened, and his eyebrows were drawn together, as he stated fearlessly, "Right here, Gotham."

"Ahhh, yes! Step forth, boy!" Gotham then placed his right claw back around Sable's neck. Griffin slowly strode past the enduring Critins. Their eyes followed him as he went along. Gotham shoved Sable forward, releasing him from his grasp as Griffin stopped before them. "I want *you* to personally deliver *my* diamond to me."

Griffin took in a deep breath through his lungs then made his way to Sable. Sable stood before him, tears still glistening about his face. The boy's eyes were locked upon the diamond as he approached. The deepened red glow of the gem illuminated Griffin's face as he stopped in front of Sable. He continued the trance the diamond seemed to have over him.

And as Gotham grew impatient, he roared, "Bring it here, human!"

Griffin reacted to his demands and looked up to the dark dragon. He gazed into the eyes of the vile beast, and as he did, Griffin asked himself, *Why? What has caused this dragon to be so evil? Why did it have to come to this?* And in that moment Griffin was gazing upon the dragon's eyes, he made an undeniably momentous discovery. *Gotham's eyes—they are the same color as the diamond.* And as soon as this epiphany left his thoughts, his mind entertained him with the image of Eden at the altar. Not only did he see Eden as clear as the air before him, but the last riddle rang in his mind as well. *"The enemy's weakness is closer to you than one may know. You must grasp it and not allow it to glow. If you can achieve this task, the Critins will prosper and be free at last."* "Sable," Griffin whispered, "that is it...that is it!"

"What is going on?" Gotham bared his enlarged fangs as saliva foamed from his mouth in his vile wrath. "I said bring the diamond to me!" Griffin then looked up to Gotham, and for the first time, it was Griffin who had a menacing look as he smirked at Gotham.

"What are you doing, my boy?" Sable questioned in dismay.

Griffin did not reply but instead wrapped both of his arms around the neck of the diamond bearer, slowly lifting the diamond off of him. As the chain cleared Sable's head, Griffin held the piece up, hanging it before his face for many moments.

"Griffin...it is over," Sable reminded.

Griffin did not react to Sable's words but, instead, continued to gaze at the red gem before him. This solitary item that he held before him had always been the key to the Critins' salvation—it was what they desperately needed to protect. This red diamond was the very reason Griffin was even in Aranwea. He revoked the memory of chasing down this mysterious red light in his backyard woods. The diamond brought this young man to the Critins, to his family, and to his undeniable legacy.

"Sable," Griffin spoke softly as Gotham began to move forward in his anger toward

Griffin and the diamond bearer, "this diamond has brought me to you...but it has deceived us, Sable."

Sable turned his head to the side in confusion. And not a moment later, Griffin obtained a tighter grip around the chain of the diamond and took a large step backward, standing before a fallen piece of a Critin stone hut.

"Seize him!" Gotham snarled as he lunged for the boy, shoving Sable out of his path, tossing him to the ground.

This dragon was fast; however, he was not fast enough. And before he could reach Griffin, the boy lifted his arm upward, and then with all the might his weary body could bring about, he thrust it into the stone.

"*Noooo!*" Gotham roared.

The diamond made impact with the solid rock, causing it to make a minute crack in it. The remaining Critin family watched in horror as their precious red diamond, now slightly broken, hung from the chain in Griffin's hand. Many of the Critins then began to tremble in terror as they prepared themselves for the worst for they *thought* this was their key to survival. Griffin released the chain, allowing the diamond to rest on the ground with the crack in it.

"What have you done, Griffin?" Sable shuddered. He was still on the ground where Gotham left him.

"Look." Griffin nodded his head in Gotham's direction.

Sable followed Griffin's gesture, and as he did, he witnessed the mighty dragon clenching his chest where his heart rested and taking in enlarged breaths of air. It was as if he had taken a great blow to his body, the kind of blow that depletes one of all air and is forced to gasp viciously. Sable made his way to his feet, never taking eye contact away from Gotham.

The dragon continued to clench his heart with his right claw, stumbling backwards. His body swayed uncontrollably as the beast roared in pain, causing smoke to arise from his large nostrils. The dragon then turned to Griffin with a remorseless look and muttered, "You!"

Griffin looked to the diamond that rested on the ground, and as he did, the tiny crack that had been made soon spread throughout the entire diamond. As the fracture dispersed, Gotham grew weaker as he released his claw from his chest and placed it on the ground, trying to keep his balance. The diamond was now severely broken as all, even the Shriekian army, watched in total disbelief at what they were witnessing.

"Could it be true?" Snolan asked as she got her four legs beneath her.

Griffin turned back to Snolan who had now made it to her feet. "Yes, Snolan," he stated. "The diamond was never the Critins' weakness...it was the Shriekians'...your brother's."

Sable walked past Gotham, who was now heaving in oxygen from the ground. The diamond bearer reached down and took the fractured gem up in his talon. He lifted it to eye level as shards of it broke in his palm. And as the pieces came off, something slipped out of the center of the diamond. Carefully, Sable used his other talon to obtain what was embedded in the gem.

Griffin stared at what Sable held before him. "What *is* that?" the boy asked.

What Sable uncovered in the diamond was thin and nearly transparent. It was black, flimsy, and only an inch in length. "This, Griffin"—Sable could barely get out the words—"this is a dragon scale."

Griffin then shifted his head toward Gotham who was panting on the dirt flooring. The dragon's eyes were half open as he appeared to be going in and out of consciousness. He took one last look at Gotham's beating red eyes before he shut them entirely. The Shriekian army all gawked at their suffering leader as they moved in a bit closer to him where he rested.

Wretch marched up the Gotham's side and screamed, "We answer to you, sir!" No movement came from the anguished creature. The Shriekian leader then bent down closer towards Gotham and sneered, "If you are *not* fit to lead this army, then I shall take over."

Gotham's eyes then opened forcefully; however, the color was not the same. It was not the deepened red that contained the evilness and wrathful hatred like before. Gotham's eyes were calm, serene, and now owned the same color of eyes that Snolan had—ocean blue.

The dragon shifted his head from side to side. He looked entirely perplexed as all gazed upon him. Getting his claws in front of him, he struggled to make it to his feet. Now standing on all fours, he softly asked, "Where is my sister? Where is Snolan?" The confused being gawked about the scene until his eyes fell upon a familiar dragon. He slowly walked to Snolan, who was in disbelief. He stood before her with concern, "Snolan, you are wounded. What has brought this on?" Snolan continued to gaze into the now-blue eyes of her brother. "Where are the others, Snolan? Where is our family?"

A tear glistened down her face as her brother spoke. This whole time, Snolan had known that Gotham was under *their* control, but she did not understand every part of it. She had not the slightest idea that the diamond controlled his every being.

Snolan was not the only one who was in disbelief. Sable sulked to himself for all this time, he had endured protecting this gem; he had finally come to the realization that it was *never* the Critins' weakness, but of the Shriekians' instead. The Critin family had obtained the diamond many, many decades ago. And somehow along the way, lines got crossed, and the true relevance of the diamond had been misinterpreted. And just as the prophecy stated, it was only the chosen one who could truly find the Shriekians' weakness and bring the Critins to their, at last, salvation. By breaking the diamond, Griffin had disarmed their spellbound leader, Gotham.

Snolan struggled to absorb all that was taking place. She shook off a few fallen tears and wept, "My brother, there are no other dragons... the Shriekians destroyed our family when we had barely begun to walk this land."

Gotham then turned to the Shriekian army and lowered his eyes in hatred. He growled at them as the army began to slowly step backward.

Snolan could scarcely speak the remainder of what she had to say. "Gotham...you have been leading the Shriekians for the past seven decades...and there are no more dragons."

"I refuse to believe this!" the infuriated dragon bellowed. Gotham then pointed his face downward, and like a wolf releasing a midnight howl, he slowly raised his head upward, and when doing so, he released a deafening wail throughout the evening sky. The sound of his roar echoed throughout the entire land of Aranwea as each sound wave grew more powerful with every second. The roar whipped past the trees and echoed throughout the valleys. It penetrated deep into the waters and shook the grounds of Aranwea like an earthquake. When the howling had subsided, all was silent. All beings in this instantaneous moment were at a standstill, taking in all that just had took place.

Gotham gazed to the skies. He held his chest high with composure, taking in more air into his lungs. The dragon again sounded a thunderous howl into the land, this time for many more moments. And when the cry finally subsided and all watched in awe at the mighty dragon, large beings began to approach in the air from the direction Griffin and Adria had flown from. They were merely shadows with expanded wings cutting through the air, closing the distance between them and all beings before the castle.

As they came closer, Griffin could make out the distinct color of the creature that flew at the front. "It is them, Adria!" Griffin ran to her side. The shadow that led the entire colony of beings was the red dragon that Adria and Griffin had come across in the cave. It was the lost dragon family of Aranwea that could only be called upon by *their* leader.

The beasts circled around the battle scene below. There were over sixty dragons that flew overhead of all different shapes and sizes. Some were large with exotic colors of purple and red. Others were smaller and owned sharp horns jutting out the top of their skulls. They were fearsome beings with glittering scales, and giant wings. As they continued to circle the battle from above, many of them released their fiery breaths into the air, showing off their prestige.

Before anyone could react, the leader of the Shriekian army demanded, "Gotham commands the dragons now!" Wretch raised his slimy fist in the air and screamed, "Silence him!" The army did as they were told. They raced past the remaining Critins to make their way to their once leader.

Gotham lowered his head and growled with hatred as all Shriekian enclosed him in a circle. "Dragons of Aranwea, your vengeance await you!" Gotham could barely get the words out before he was overtaken by waves of Shriekian beasts, biting, gnawing and tearing their way toward him, bringing him to the ground beneath their fury.

The dragons then dispersed. Some dove straight toward the battle below, ripping the Shriekian off the back of their leader beneath them. Others landed to the ground and released deadly flames, engulfing the vile beings. Adria gathered up the Critin youngsters who had been brought to the battle scene and took them back into the castle for safety as the remaining Critins fought side by side with the dragons.

Arrows continued to rain, and fire did not cease. Griffin found his shortbow and quiver he had placed on the ground and released his uncontrollable wrath upon them with the last bit of energy his body could bring about. The red dragon that Griffin and Adria found in the cave had a large group of Shriekian creatures trapped between her and three other dragons. The Shriekian attempted to dodge around the enclosed area, but when they did, another dragon would step in their way. The red dragon stepped closer and closer to the shuddering beasts as they began to shove at one another, hissing in sheer panic. Meeka, the red dragon, spoke, "You have harmed our kind many, many decades ago—it is *your* time to suffer!" She then opened her jaws to full capacity as the Shriekian winced in fear and covered their alien-like faces with their webbed hands. The dragons around her did the same, and in that sudden moment, all dragons around the vile monsters set free an inferno so scorching and so powerful the dragons themselves had to take a step back for the flames greatly heated their scales. The Shriekian screeched in agony as the flames burned their rubbery skin, overpowering them in their inescapable mortality.

This time, the dragons and the remaining Critins were too much for the Shriekian to compete with. And as the war raged on and Shriekian upon Shriekian was brought down, Griffin knew the tides had turned. And even though the Critin race had suffered a great loss and many of their family members had sacrificed their lives for freedom, this was the dawning of a new era. And in a place where *so* much life was being lost, Griffin saw existence before him. This was the war to put all else to rest. The final, inevitable, and predestined battle that would be the rebirthing of this entire land was taking place before this boy's eyes.

The Critins had waited so long for this day to come, and it finally had. Not only the Critins gained the revenge they rightfully deserved, but the dragons did as well. The Shriekian had nearly wiped all Critins *and* dragons from all hope of survival. This was the Shriekians' turn to perish. It was their time to feel the suffering that these two races had felt due to them. It was the Shriekians' vile souls that drove them to do such wretched things, and now these two colonies had come together with a fistful of vengeance that surely would not end until they saw that each and every Shriekian had met their doom.

LIBERTY IN ARANWEA

The red diamond had been broken. The gem that the Critins had protected for so long had deceived these beings nearly seven decades. One might wonder how such a thing could be possible and how the diamond controlled Gotham's every action. The answer lies in Gotham's youth. Gotham had been tempted by the Shriekians when he was a young dragon, and he did willingly go to them.

But what the Critins, and even Gotham did not know, was that when the Shriekians' leader at the time, Cyrus, found this baby dragon, he took something *from* Gotham. Cyrus stole one of Gotham's dragon scales and embedded it in a red gem, casting a curse on the diamond, along with his hatred and ability to rule the Shriekian race. When it came to humans, the power the Shriekians owned was *nearly* impossible for them to defy, but dragons, on the other hand, were not so easily convinced. Cyrus knew that in order for this dragon to truly be consumed in the enemy's power, he had to set Gotham in a trancelike state. And that was the sole purpose of the red diamond the Critins came into possession of. It was never the Critins' inevitable weakness. They were led to believe *that* by the Shriekian; it was the Shriekians' weakness in itself. When the gem had been broken, and the scale had been removed, Gotham withdrew from this trance and gained back his true essence.

When the war was finally claimed to be victorious by the Critins, they rejoiced with tears of gladness and also despair. Despair for the many lives that had been taken away from them and gladness for they could at last claim their land of Aranwea and live in harmony with the remaining dragons. Once Gotham grasped the reality of the Shriekians' deception over him, he exhausted every last ounce of himself into diminishing the Shriekian.

All dragons circled around their suffering leader they had been waiting for. And before his eyes were laid to rest and death overcame his weary and battered body, he asked his sister something that he knew she might not be able to fulfill. And that question was if *she* would now rule the lost dragon race of Aranwea. Snolan, who had convinced herself there were no more dragons left in Aranwea, had a substantial decision to make. That decision was either to stay with the Critins and continue to be their ever so protecting castle guardian, or leave with the dragons, and rule her own kind.

Griffin, Adria, and Snolan sat along the water's edge that ran through the Roggon forest. The once stream was now a thriving river that flowed through Aranwea due to the destruction of the Shriekian domain. The Shriekians' murky depths were no longer inhabited since the demise of the vile creatures, and with that, the rivers greatly thrived and were able to flourish to their full potential. Griffin tossed a pebble into the flowing waters as Snolan lay in the grass, allowing her white scales to dance in the afternoon sun. "Snolan?" Adria turned to the dragon as she brushed her brown locks out of her eyes. "Will you regret your decision?"

The dragon grinned and she looked to Adria. "My dear," Snolan spoke, "Meeka will make a fine leader." Snolan then brought herself to her all fours, shaking off some loose grass. "My lost dragon race that I have been in search of for all these decades have finally been found, and if I wish it, I can go to them whenever I please." She paused for a moment and looked to Griffin, who was now down by the banks, searching for more rocks to toss in the rapids. "But my family is here with the Critins, here with you, and here with Griffin. It shall remain that way until the end of my time." Snolan stretched her neck out to Adria and nuzzled her scaly cheek against hers. "I will let you two be. Sable says he has prepared something for me...do you know what this is about, Adria?"

Adria turned her flushed face away from Snolan as a grin crept across her mouth. She replied in a sarcastic manner, "I have no idea what you are talking about, Snolan."

"Adria!" Snolan was exasperated.

Adria hastily flung her hands toward the direction of the castle. "You will find out soon enough!"

Snolan then rolled her blue eyes and bounded off toward the castle.

Adria strolled down to the riverside where Griffin stood. She gently took his hand in hers as Griffin turned to face her. "Did Snolan leave?" Griffin wondered.

"Yes." Adria smiled, gazing at the passing water below. "Sable's presenting the new corridor in the castle made just for her." Adria giggled a bit. "She has no idea he has been preparing this for her."

Griffin tossed the rock that he had been holding with his left hand into the river. Shifting his head back to her, he said, "Well, Snolan rightfully deserves it if you ask me. A place to rest to call her own, a place to stay."

"I could not agree more." Adria then paused for a moment as if hesitant to pursue her following words. "Did you...did you mean what you said, Griffin?" Her eyes found his as the boy shyly looked away.

"What...what do you mean? Did I mean what I said about what?" Griffin could feel his heartbeat within his chest.

Adria stepped in front of him, taking his other hand in hers as well. "When we were surrounded by the Shriekian, and we thought there was no hope left...you said something."

Griffin continued to gaze off in the other direction as he fought back his smile and his face became flushed with redness. "I do not remember such a thing, Adria," he replied in sarcasm. Finally, he shifted his eyes back to her.

"I think you remember *exactly* what you said, Griffin Dominic. And I want you to admit it!" Adria let go of his hands and placed her palms upon her hips. "Well...?" she pressed.

Griffin reluctantly smiled and reached for Adria's arm, pulling her closer to him once more. He began, "I do, Adria. I do remember what I said." Adria's face lit up as he continued his words. "And...and I meant every bit of it and still do. This land was meant for us to find. We were meant to share it together, Adria."

Usually the boy would shyly look away, but this time his eyes did not leave hers. "Looking back when I saw the red light in my backyard woods, my first night flight, finding the prophecy, I cannot believe what has happened and how everything has changed. Ever since I was little, I knew I was meant to do something more in life. But this? This, Adria, was much more than I had in mind." He chuckled a bit, holding her even tighter as she rested her head upon his chest. "This all is truly unbelievable, and I would not want my life to have taken any other path. Here with the Critins is where I belong. Here with you, Adria, is where I will stay."

They held each other under the arms of the comforting redwood trees in the land they could now claim as their home, the land of Aranwea.

LIVE

listen|imagine|view|experience

AUDIO BOOK DOWNLOAD INCLUDED WITH THIS BOOK!

In your hands you hold a complete digital entertainment package. In addition to the paper version, you receive a free download of the audio version of this book. Simply use the code listed below when visiting our website. Once downloaded to your computer, you can listen to the book through your computer's speakers, burn it to an audio CD or save the file to your portable music device (such as Apple's popular iPod) and listen on the go!

How to get your free audio book digital download:

1. Visit www.tatepublishing.com and click on the e|LIVE logo on the home page.
2. Enter the following coupon code:
   d5e8-8759-ba20-e80a-59ad-1c7a-7700-d49e
3. Download the audio book from your e|LIVE digital locker and begin enjoying your new digital entertainment package today!